SCHOOL OF BREAKING

Cover art by artist from Slovakia, name unknown

School of Breaking copyright © 2014, 2018 Alesya Grigorovitch

ISBN: 978-0-9837647-1-7

Table of Contents

Part I

Emile was born in the heart of Prague and there she spent her first years of life. She remembered nothing from those early days except for a neighbor she used to play with, a girl named Lillian, who streaked through her mind from time to time in flashes of blonde and blue. These vague recollections were all that remained of a life's first iteration crossed out as if never written, for when Emile was five, her parents picked up their young family and moved to as different a life as possible. They relocated to Locronan, a tiny village on the edge of France that faced toward the Atlantic and away from the rest of the world. Its two hundred-strong population spread out along the coast, bleeding inland in widely spaced tributaries of farm houses that spiraled through clumps of storied woods into a tightly nested town carved out in the thirteenth century and remaining little changed until that day. Against such serenity, Emile watched the Atlantic's blue waves roll in day and night. She was born in Prague, but it was in Locronan that her spirit grew.

Her daily walks to the village center from their cottage felt as old as the forest they cut through, whose gnarled trees stemmed from earth old as the path she trod.

They were rooted so deeply they grew their annual mass as a matter of boredom, laughing at the passing world from the wisdom of their own slowed time, a wisdom that wordlessly seeped into Emile. She emerged from the trees to a wide, low hill overlooking the sea, always pausing to behold this ever-changing picture of continuity that still awed her after ten years.

The Locronans' unguarded openness enmeshed the little family into the fabric of village life quickly. Before one season ended Emile's parents were raising crops and commiserating over the weather patterns as if they had been at it their whole lives. Little Emile took to village life as if she'd come home, acquiring a passion for playing chansons on the lute, for tending to the garden, for strolling through the woods picking mushrooms and berries, for frequenting the market. Never were her seaside walks sweeter than on those Sunday mornings when she carried her empty basket and a few coins into town. The tip of Locronan's old church emerged at the hill's crest, giving way to the stone body, the cobblestone courtyard, and the noise and bustle of people mingling below. Emile chatted leisurely and moved with an unhurried gait like the rest. She herself had become embedded into Locronan's life like the stones that made their world, held within the earth like the elder trees, and this state afforded her a sense of deepest satisfaction.

It was a town of kind, hardworking people leading simple lives. Surrounded by such, Emile grew up to be so herself. By age fifteen not the smallest grain of manipulation or deceit had besmirched the setting mold of her character. Stories from Paris of atrocities against fellow humans trickled in from her schoolmates' savvier urban cousins, always told with an awe surrounding such intrigues, which nobody could believe and which Emile herself could never conceive of until she heard them. She pushed their notions away. Nothing of that world appealed to her. She recalled almost nothing of her life before in the world beyond, but she instinctively knew that she lived a life people spent decades searching for and stumbled into, often by luck, at the end of a long and meandering road.

The inland world reached them through a swamp of slowed time, but Emile's own growth moved along unimpeded. After ten idyllic years had come to pass, she stood on a cusp with childhood's waning moon behind her and the glimmer of a next era beckoning inexorably on. She spent these strange days facing the ocean in a kind of meditation; she had no desire for the wider world at her back. She already knew where she belonged.

Then as suddenly as they'd arrived, Emile's father

announced their abrupt return to Prague; Emile would start boarding school that summer and her parents would take more prospective jobs in the city.

She could not process this ripping out. She could retrace every archway in the village blindly, could feel every stone beneath her fingers like an extension of her own body. The villagers were her family; to leave them behind was to leave behind herself.

But boxes were packed and the home that had made her was emptied. They left on a morning when the leaves were just unfurling on wet branches, and in three days' time had crammed themselves into an empty rowhouse on a street with no trees in sight on which to watch spring's progression.

Weak sunlight crept in through the splintered wood frames of her new bedroom windows that first morning. Emile sprung from her unfamiliar mattress and ran still half asleep to the front door, throwing it open. She met dry bricks and a silent street. The smell of a foreign city hit her face, where it fought the smell of the sea still lodged in her nose, not yet wafted away.

She ached to refill the fading stores of that salty smell, but her parents offered her an oppositely facing solution.

"Why don't you visit the parks, darling? There's a lovely one nearby, Malešice," said her mother in the kitchen where she brewed coffee and examined a map.

She handed the map to Emile, who studied it for several minutes and left it by the front door to set out with free hands and a free mind. She passed sad little plots of land sprouting limp grass under loud groups of playing children and looked halfheartedly around for Lillian. Even if her friend still lived here, she wasn't likely to run into her in this never ending sprawl. Emile had passed more than five times Locronan's population already just on her way to one of the city's smaller parks.

She abandoned the disappointing green and made her way on a long street into Old Town, steering into an alley of towering stone structures flaunting intricate frescoes, singling herself out as a tourist with her turning head. When she stepped out to the Main Square, she stopped. The grandeur was impossible to take in at once. Dirt black gothic buildings loomed over the crowd like stone shadows. The sinking behemoth of Our Lady Before Týn alone consumed more stone than all of Locronan. It dawned on Emile that ten of Locronan's church were dwarfed inside it.

The crowd swarmed around her as she stood still and though it was a mess of noise, nobody paused to speak.

Stories of Paris echoed in her mind as she watched the line-mouth, locked-eye faces pass each other in coldness, apathy at best, through the magnificent maze, where, for the first time since their arrival, curiosity reared its head above nostalgia.

She ventured smoothly into adjoining Žižkov where uneven rows of houses in staggered lines replaced Old Town's grandeur. Late afternoon light cast distorting shadows over the cobblestones and weathered walls. It was unexpectedly quiet, the windows of cafes darkened beneath artfully painted wooden signs. Emile recalled that it was Sunday.

The first streetlight came on when the sky turned cerulean. Emile turned around at last, satisfied and full with her new impressions, to retrace her steps, benchmarking the way back by houses. The shadow maze playing upon buildings had been rearranged by the dimmer light. One uncertain turn by its markings led her onto a quiet street that she could not tell for familiar or new.

The sky now deepened to ink above her and the shadows disappeared. Only little pockets of light glowed under the streetlights. There hadn't been another soul down the length of any street since the lamps had come on, and this street was no different. She panicked, turning in place, primed for any sign of a human face.

From a dark patch between two streetlights, a bright little spark flashed like a sputtering streetlamp, but that it was not. It was moving. It was a lamp, she realized, swinging in the hand of a tiny, darkness-obscured girl whom it took Emile a moment to observe was zigzagging from door to door, bearing strongly the air of searching. When she passed under a streetlamp, the light illuminated a long, midnight blue nightgown covered in silver stars that twinkled briefly like a riddle. Pulled irresistibly, Emile sped after her.

The little wanderer never slowed. Whenever Emile got so close she could trace the patterns in the old swinging lantern, the girl plunged into a patch of darkness that retarded Emile as she paused. The darkness had no effect on the little girl, and she reemerged clearly in the next patch of light putting meters between them once more. Emile lost track of the turns and alleys they took with every bend they rounded. But she rounded one into a narrow street and found herself truly alone. She was sure the girl had run here and the narrow street was long, but her lantern light was nowhere in sight. The street was almost pitch dark and silent, devoid of the soft patter of footsteps she had run to like a drum.

Emile stalked slowly among the houses, looking for a just closed door. She found only unbudging black window panes.

A very faint, almost lazy light emerged just behind a jutting wall between two unevenly aligned houses, the larger one sticking into the street, hiding a smaller, recessed building that looked distinctly like it was there first. The light came from a lantern fitted lopsidedly on its nondescript front,hidden from the street by its neighbors. Its dim gold burn deepened the lines of the heavy oak door it crowned.

Dark window curtains betrayed no sign of activity within. She pressed her ear to the door, so old its bottom corners were rounded and worn over pressed dirt and pebbles, and thought she heard faint laughter behind it. Hesitantly, she pushed it open. To her surprise, it yielded.

Emile thought she had walked into someone's living room, but the many round tables and the mahogany bar on the far end said otherwise. The raucous little space was filled with people in lurid costumes that spilled their breasts and rolls as they bent around and hugged, laughing riotously and clanking their glasses among the dim light of many ensconced candles. In the back, a jester fell drunkenly over one of the tables.

"Close it!" came a guttural roar from somewhere in that vicinity.

The door closed with a soft thud behind her. Long spiderleg-like fingers rested on it, belonging to the strangest

8

man Emile had ever seen, seeming to stand guard but appearing an inefficient choice to defend a bar. Tall and extremely thin, he wore a toneless brown-gray tunic that hung off his shoulders like a loose curtain to match the lank hair on his head that looked unwashed. In his corpse-like face, sunken eyes like fathomless unlit tunnels met Emile's, but without a word he retreated to the wall and resumed watching over the scene, speaking with no one and maintaining a straight mouth.

Emile moved slowly past the tables piled wide and high with empty glasses. No one seemed bothered by her presence save for one group of four heavily ornamented women gossiping deeply around a table near the middle, who gave her pointed looks as she walked by them and continued to watch her progression all the way to the bar.

"Catch that!" cried the same voice who'd ordered the door closed, and from the bar itself the stocky jester dove to the floor after his fallen hat, scrambling for it like a wild boar. The women paused in their conversation to turn to and sneer at the sight.

Emile had never seen such beauties; their painted faces shimmered in the ambient light and they wore lustrous velvet corsets that brazenly presented nature's gifts like fruits on a platter. Three were pretty in an earthy way, but one was exceptional; dark and regal, she possessed a queenly air. Rich dark hair cascaded down her back in shining, unrepressed waves, and a voluptuous figure that was the envy of any woman made her the essence of femininity. But it was the clever, aristocratic face atop her long, elegant neck, framed with long arching eyebrows over dark liquid eyes that lent her her peculiar mystique. She gave the jester the hardest look of all, but she herself was no saint; a collection of empty glasses in varying sizes cowed her companions', and Emile had the distinct impression that she was using every ounce of willpower to keep from joining the jester on the floor.

Emile recalled her mother's soft brown waves and eyes, pleasant but muted, and her modest shirts and dresses, nothing like this woman who flaunted her beauty like a rose in full bloom.

Emile sidled up to an empty stool at the bar and with difficulty climbed aboard. She sat alone for a minute. Nobody in the bar approached her and the one man operating behind the counter was tied up with a few other men down at the other end. He turned his attention to her after extricating himself from their conversation.

"Can I help you?" he asked in warm tones that came forth from the tangled beard blocking all expression of the face underneath. Emile detected a smile below the hair, echoed in the brown eyes. Or perhaps it was a smirk.

"Yes, please," she cleared her throat before formally declaring, "I'm lost."

"Lost?" he repeated slowly, stretching out the word as if it were a new concept. She leaned more toward smirk; there was a slight mock to his tone. "Are you new here?"

"Yes.... Well... yes and no," she grew thoughtful both of the question and of how to endear this stranger who seemed to be fighting the urgency of her need to get home. "I'm from here."

"You are?" he leaned both elbows against the counter in earnest and new curiosity twitched under the beard. "Then why are you lost?"

"We moved away when I was very young and we just moved back."

"Where did you move to?"

"Locronan. Do you know of it?"

He shook his head naively.

"It's a little village, and it's over a thousand kilometers away."

"Which direction?" he asked.

"France. On the westernmost part, right on the ocean," Emile said, succumbing to the sudden memory of the waves.

"Do you miss it?" the bartender asked as if he already knew.

"More than I've ever missed anything. But I can't go back now," she looked at the opaque wood barely shining in some spots, feeling at once lonely in a place so different from the one contained in whole within her heart.

The bartender's sympathy shone through. "Take heart. You're young. Everything is still ahead of you."

"Years of boarding school are ahead of me," Emile said and he made a sympathetic noise. "But after that, I'll return."

"We'll keep this seat warm for you," he said.

"Wh – I meant I'll return to Locronan!"

The bartender chuckled.

"I don't even know where I am," Emile looked around the bar once more. "And I don't know how to get home."

"Where *is* home? Locronan, or here?" the bartender posed, fumbling around behind the counter again.

"Locronan," she said immediately, "...I think... I don't know anymore."

"Well, then! I think we've found the problem!" he

exclaimed. "This should help you sort it out," he set down a glass of something bright snake green he'd been concocting as they'd talked. "This will quench your unbearable thirst. Or make it worse."

Emile just noticed how parched her throat was after the chase.

"Try it. I've already made a few tonight."

At the reassurance of spotting a few green glints around the room, Emile took a sip. It was like nothing she'd tasted before, sweet and pungent and powerful.

"Good?" the bartender asked, the smile behind his beard now wide.

"I can't tell. It's interesting," Emile pondered as her face unsquinched.

"That's better than a simple 'good'. Keep trying," he nodded.

Emile sipped slowly, watching the scene unfold through the green in her hand and watching the bar became a golden blur above the ever lowering liquor line, enveloping the crowd that hung suspended in this bubble with no tomorrow in sight that she could tell. Emile wondered, for a moment, if she herself didn't lack a tomorrow.

"What do you miss about Locronan?" the bartender

asked, sipping an amber drink at a similar pace.

Emile thought a long moment, a process the drink helped with. "I miss the trees. I miss walking along and hearing the ocean. I miss our house. I miss the town and its old buildings. I miss the market and stopping and seeing everyone. I miss the people, most of all. All the people in Locronan are simple and kind and they'll never fool you. People here... well, nobody smiles."

"I smiled at you," said the bartender.

"Aren't you supposed to smile at people?" she asked.

A harsh laugh broke out right next to her.

"She's right. Do your job!" a fat finger wagged at the young man.

The jester from across the bar had climbed onto the stool next to her, the dirty hat firmly back on his head with sardonically jingling bells hanging off of limp purple, green, and yellow felt arms. The stench from him was unbearable. Emile politely leaned away. He eyed her with tiny bloodshot eyes that had trouble keeping her in focus.

"Do I smell that bad?" the bum said in no shy manner and sniffed near the armpit of his days' unwashed shirt. "My apologies!" he tapped Emile's arm and almost fell of his stool trying to scoot away from her.

"Who brought her here?" he barked at the bartender as he straightened out.

"I got lost and stumbled in," Emile said quickly, but the bartender went about serving others, the bum's harsh tones simply rolling off his back.

The bum gave another barking laugh.

"I stumble in here every night! Who are you?"

"Emile."

"And who is that?"

"I – don't know – "

"You don't know? Then maybe you're one of *us*," said the bum, the jester's hat crooked but still miraculously on his head.

"She's not," said the bartender. "She came here by accident."

"Nobody comes here by accident," the bum brushed away abrasively. "We must get to the bottom of it. Get her another!" he ordered.

"I can't. My parents will worry," said Emile as a glass appeared before her.

"Your parents are already worried. What's the harm if the damage is already done?"

"He has a point," the bartender agreed.

"I don't want to be drunk!" cried Emile.

"You mean you don't want to end up like *me*," the drunk bared an ear-to-ear grin showing yellow crooked teeth.

Emile had no reply and he laughed again. The bartender and two others, a man significantly larger than either the bum or the bartender and one of the women from the table of four, a blonde, laughed at the bum, but their laughter surrounded Emile.

"Nothing to worry about, girlie. You're not our kind," said the woman, whose laughter had been more of a prolonged snort.

"I'll tell you," the bum prodded the woman's arm with a fat, beer-free finger, "there are only two kinds: those who see with their eyes open, and those who see with their eyes closed." Then he leaned his face closer to Emile's, and said "Tell me, which kind are you?"

People were flailing and falling over all around the bar. Saliva sprayed out of their mouths as they took deep gulps and almost spat them back out from spurts of laughter. Breasts halfway hung out of blouses, urged fully out by hungry hands and drunken smiles. A table nearly toppled over, almost carrying a group of three with it, righted amid roars just before breaking and tilted now the other way. Emile flinched at the shrieks and thuds.

"I – I don't know. This isn't my place," she said, looking around at the spectacle of debauchery and keeping close to herself as the large man threw a beer down his gullet and the woman gave him a look.

"Don't pay him mind," said the blonde with as much sympathy in her voice as in her eyes. "Forget this little mishap and run back to mommy and daddy."

"She doesn't want to run back to mommy and daddy," the drunk cut in.

"She wants to run back to Locronan," said the bartender, and Emile jumped at the casual outing of her privately divulged thoughts. "The most beautiful place in the world," he went on.

"Nonsense. If you wanna hear about some beautiful places – !" said the bum.

"The toilet bowl and the floor?" asked the large man to respondent laughter.

"Right *here*!" the bum took the bar in with his hands. The three others and a few surrounding patrons laughed again.

"Maybe Locorn has the prettiest trees, but we have the prettiest *people*," the bum threw his arms around the woman and man, who quickly slipped out from under his sweat-stained sleeves. With the tipping table stable again, their little crowd had consolidated all the attention now. The man by the doorway stood there still, participating only by watching them. Emile involuntarily scoffed.

"You don't think we're pretty?" the bum feigned hurt.

"Let her go home. There's pretty people there, I'm sure," said the blonde.

"She doesn't know how to get home," said the bartender.

"Few do," the bum interjected. "What I want to know is how she got here."

"Leave it alone, you. If she was one of ours, she'd already be drunk," the burly man keeping guard between Emile and the bum commented.

"It'll go to waste," the bartender winked at her and nodded to the untouched second glass.

"No it won't," the large man picked it up. "She wants to go home, so let's help her go home," he said, lifting her easily from her chair by her upper arm and pulling her along toward the front door as nobody stopped him and the remaining crowd watched from their stools, a few lending jeers along the way and the man at the door as passive as he'd been all night.

The old oak door slammed shut in her face. Emile stood in the middle of the street again, as dark and empty as before she'd stepped in. The effect of the drink still coursed through her. She pressed her hand to the door that had ejected her; its silence did not invite her back inside. She turned around and began to stumble along the dark streets taking best guesses, and after a few easy turns emerged onto a main street she recognized immediately.

"Where have you been?" her stricken father demanded when he answered the door with her mother's blanched face poking out from behind him.

"I got lost."

"Where did you – ? Are you drunk?" he sniffed.

"I went into a bar to get directions."

"And?"

"They gave me a drink. I didn't know what it was and I was thirsty – "

Her parents drew back, appalled.

"Emile!"

"What bar is this!" her father demanded.

"It didn't have a name. I swear! There was no sign anywhere on it," she exclaimed to their disbelieving faces.

"Emile, what were you thinking?" her mother cried.

"It could've been a secret society! It could've – you never know!"

"It wasn't a secret society," Emile said, though she could not truly be certain of this. Only now was the sober reflection of her actions finally setting in. It was most unlike her, to run after a light, to take a drink from a stranger, to divulge her private concerns to a room. The more minutes that passed between her and her family standing in the hallway and the strange encounter, the more Emile looked back on the event in wonder.

Her father was determined to solve the mystery of the nameless bar, but nobody, not even those who had lived in Prague their whole lives, had heard of such a place. Emile attempted to find it again herself, but her parents imposed a strict curfew and by daylight the Zizkov streets were friendly and open. She stood no chance of finding it in those hours when all looked different and it was impossible to get lost. Soon, the strange bar and its clownish patrons went the way of Locronan and the previous ten years of her life, becoming more of a dream than a memory. Emile was no longer even certain the encounter had happened. She might have dreamed or hallucinated it.

Other concerns took the mystery's place. Her start at

Alvarus Academy, the prestigious institution her parents had attended when they were her age and had each met the person they were going to marry, was approaching in a few short weeks and Emile had no time to wander around in search of secret bars as she sat in her room or the nearby park reading from the numerous textbooks her parents had bought her in preparation.

The drowsiness set in by theorems and problem sets was a perfect soil for idyllic daydreams that recycled Locronan's essence for a backdrop and filled in the main characters by drawing on her mother's recollections of her own time at Alvarus.

"It's a *beautiful* little town. An old castle overlooks it from the hill. Your father and I used to walk there all the time. It's where we had our first kiss," she remembered pleasantly. "You'll love it."

Under the April sun, Emile 's brain, having eaten up the tales, spun visions of its own accord of romantic walks through lush green forests, perhaps accompanied by a young, studious boy who would discuss the book they were reading in one of the many beautiful gardens. It was with such pleasant fantasies to gild the unknown that she boarded the train to Alvarus on a fresh morning in the middle of spring.

"Remember, we're less than three hours away," her

mother said as she hugged her goodbye.

Emile watched the pair of them from her window. They were the salt of the earth, her mother angelic, with a face that was a mixture of worry and acceptance, her father tall and handsome, with a stern but gentle expression under a coif of rich brown hair. He kept his arm around her mother as they stood side by side like statuettes and watched the train depart....

Emile fluidly lapsed into her well rehearsed daydreams as the forest sped by, unaware of the sun dipping behind the leafy canopy until it shone through only in sputtering rays. Jolting out of her alternate life and into the quiet train compartment, Emile sat up to undo the cramps in her body, figuring their imminent arrival.

They had stopped in a station where two thin black spires from a distant cathedral poked the blue and orange sky like needles.

"Brno!" cried an attendant repeatedly, walking through the compartments. Emile fell back in her seat and watched the mass exodus off the train that left her with only one ragged-looking man for company, deep asleep in the seat diagonally across from her.

Too wide awake to daydream, Emile examined her

slumbering neighbor. His light brown hair pleasantly faded to gray around the temples, but he resembled none of the recently departed crowd in their neat suits, slick briefcases, and refolded newspapers or bestselling novels. He instead donned a shabby coat covered in dirt and stains, and beside him lay a shapeless beige bag, equally tattered and worn. She wondered where he was headed.

The sun had sunk too close to the horizon for a three hour train ride. She pressed her face to the glass; not a hint of so much as a village appeared all the way to the darkening horizon. Worried, she gently poked her companion.

"Excuse me," she said as he jumped up and gained his bearings.

"Yes?"

"Do you know what time it is?"

"Six," he checked the old watch wrapped around his thin wrist on a tattered leather band.

"Six?" Emile jumped back. They were due to have arrived an hour ago.

"Have I missed the stop to Loket?" she panicked.

The man furrowed his brows as if he couldn't understand her question.

"I'm on my way to the Academy. We were supposed to arrive – "

"Ah, are you a student?" he brightened, examining her clothes and her suitcase. "But of course you are. Yes, no need to worry, we're on the way to the school," he smiled.

"How much longer?" Emile asked. It was nearing twilight.

"Not long," he assured. "It's easy from the station, you could find it with your eyes closed. Just walk toward the hill. It sits on top," he said.

"By the castle?"

"*In* the castle!"

"You're sure?" she asked, confused. That seemed a detail her mother wouldn't fail to mention.

"Oh, yes," he smiled as if he understood every student's dream. "Amazing, no?"

Twilight had almost fallen by the time they reached the little town. Pillars bordered the station's open, hexagonal hall where the remaining travelers scattered like rays and Emile, a stranger, was soon left without even her train companion. There stood the hill clear ahead, just like he'd said, and, getting a firm grip on her suitcase, she began the slow march up to Alvarus.

Perhaps her mother had been saving the very best. The town was otherwise just as she had described: bigger than Locronan and much smaller than Prague, quaint and lovely, and indeed overlooked by an enormous castle. Sandy cobblestone wound into a dense little labyrinth of cozy cafes, lit bars, quiet houses, and closed shops that Emile passed on the way and very much in the shadow of the distant hill's great old crown. Its light hovered like the North Star until at last the upward sloping cobblestone ended at a flagstone pathway climbing steeply upwards, bordered by trees whose crowns abloom in spring's zenith fell like dark blankets below a darker sky. An iron gate set into the low stone wall was left wide open, and, dragging her luggage awkwardly up unmaintained steps, Emile walked through to an old stone house awaiting with an open door.

She was alone in what looked like the main hall. Cursing the train that made her late, Emile set down her bags in a corner and went around the grounds in search of anyone, following a faint collection of noise that hit both sides of her head with equal strength. It was behind the house, in a large garden very like the kind she'd imagined she'd find there, lit softly for the evening by lanterns, did she see someone, a girl around her size with her back to her sitting still on a bench. The sheet of shining blonde hair lit an immediate spark.

"Lillian!?" Emile cried in disbelief before she could stop herself and remember that there were thousands of girls her age who had blonde hair.

The girl turned abruptly at the sound and Emile beheld light eyes and soft freckles in the garden light.

"*Emile?*" Lillian seemed even more surprised by their reunion. Her wide blue eyes opened even wider at the apparition of her beaming old friend who ran to hug her.

"Is it really you!?" both asked at once.

"It is!" Emile exclaimed. "Are you a student here, too?"

Lillian laughed. "Of course. Why else would I be here?"

"Of course," Emile shook her head. "I just can't believe it. It's been so long and across the world we ended up at the same school. I never once imagined I'd see you here!"

"Neither did I," said Lillian curiously. "I never thought your parents would send you *here.*"

"Why not?" Emile faltered.

"It's just so far from you."

"We moved back to Prague this year," Emile explained.

"From where?"

"Locronan. It's a little village all the way in Brittany. Remember when we parted? That's where we went. We stayed there for ten years."

"You've lived in France?" Lillian's interest spiked.

"I grew up there," Emile nodded eagerly. "Oh, it's so beautiful, Lillian. All the buildings in our town are hundreds of years old and it's right on the ocean. There's farms and forests everywhere, and everyone knows everyone. You would've loved it."

"That sounds lovely. What about Paris? Is it as beautiful?"

"It's the exact opposite. Crowded and dirty and big."

"I heard it's *huge*," said Lillian. "Do you know how many people?"

"Too many!"

Lillian grinned. "Why's that?"

"When you have so many people crammed together, they start tricking each other. People said in Paris someone could be getting robbed in broad daylight and no one would do anything about it! They would just walk right by! In Locronan, if that happened, the whole town would be standing behind you. But that's why it never happened, I guess."

"You've never been to Paris?" Lillian asked.

"No. My parents had no interest in going."

"But weren't you curious?"

Emile shrugged. "Everything I heard about it made it sounded depressing and rotten. To be honest, I could never understand what people found so appealing about it."

"Variety," Lillian answered.

"I was happy in Locronan. But my parents wanted to move back and for me to come here. They were students here."

"Your parents went *here*?" Lillian sounded like she found it hard to believe.

Emile nodded. "Only it took longer to get here than they said it would. Did you take a train from Prague?"

"No. We left Prague not long after your family."

"To where?"

"Here," Lillian said. "I've been waiting to go here my whole life," she looked around the grounds as around her kingdom. "I was made for this school."

"Are... we the only students?" asked Emile to the quiet.

Lillian laughed. "Of course not! The rest went on a tour, I just know my way around. They're probably back for dinner by now. The teachers will be introducing themselves," her eyes lit up at the thought and she jumped off the bench, leading the way back in at a quick pace. Emile followed Lillian, stumbling over the path and struggling to keep up, into a noisy dining hall where a long, heavy wooden table – an entire ancient tree sliced lengthwise in half and varnished – sat in the middle like a two ton behemoth that hadn't budged in centuries. Fifty or so people crowded around it, most of them Emile and Lillian's age save for the far end, where a handful of older adults grouped together, engaged in rapt conversation.

"This is the entire school?" Emile asked of the intimate gathering.

Lillian nodded. Emile took a seat across from her and beside a dirty blonde boy with his back to her and his front entertaining a couple of girls on his other side. Lillian had commenced chatting to the girl next to her, an engaging creature with dark hair and bright eyes.

"Jesa," the girl introduced herself to Emile, not quite catching the attention of the boy next to her as they shook hands for the first time.

"Emile came all the way from Locronan, over a thousand kilometers away," said Lillian before Emile could qualify the story.

"Is that a backwards village in the middle of nowhere

with two hundred people and a town latrine?" the boy next to her whipped around and asked upon seeing Emile.

"How did you know that?" Emile asked, offended.

The burst of laughter broke the sharp, mischievous expression that had awaited her reaction.

Emile blushed. "I meant how did you know it was a village."

"Easy. I've never heard the name before."

"You know enough places to tell?" she asked dubiously.

"I've *been* to enough places to tell. I'm pretty worldly."

"Have you been to Locronan?"

"No. I usually go to places where there's something to see."

"There's plenty to see there!" Emile scoffed.

"It's in France," said Lillian.

"Oh, *oui*?" said the boy. "Near Paris?"

"Emile isn't a fan of Paris," Lillian said.

"Of course not," said the boy. "I was about to say you reminded me of a neighbor I had there, but on second thought, not at all."

"You lived there?" asked Jesa as the other two girls tuned

in to listen as the boy launched into a story from his time there.

Emile ignored this and diverted her attention to the end of the table. With a shock she saw that in the headmaster's chair sat none other than the dirty bum from the bar she had stumbled into many weeks ago. He'd foregone his jester's hat to bare a coif of ordinary brown hair and presided commandingly over his peers and pupils. On his right Emile recognized the haunting, sunken-eyed man from the bar's entrance and on his left the brunette beauty, dressed more modestly but no less evocatively.

A chink of the headmaster's glass interrupted the boy's story and all turned to face him as he stood. Though not a very large man, his broad shoulders and open chest lent him an expansive presence that filled the space, while sobriety gave him a shrewd, clever countenance that watched them with sharp eyes.

"Good evening!" he boomed, silencing the last voices. "Welcome to the Skola Lom, or, as some of you may know it, the School of Breaking. I am Godfrey, your headmaster."

Emile reeled as the students around her clapped and cheered.

"Only a few promising souls are selected to receive an

education unique in the world," Godfrey continued when the applause died down. "With the help of my capable staff, I will teach you how to survive everything life hands you, and at the end you will have the certificate to prove it." He paused to let the words sink in, to let them feel the space and prepare for what came next. "However," he surveyed each student individually, and when his eyes met Emile's it was not a look of recognition but of examination, as if assessing her capabilities , "to maintain the inimitable value of our degree, we must be a stringent institution. If you fail three classes at the time of your evaluation, you will receive nothing, not even a second chance, and be ejected from the school that very instant."

Nobody spoke, until –

"Where would we go if that happened?" asked one boy farthest from the headmaster. Emile, Lillian, Jesa, the boy, and every other student at the table turned their heads to view the asker, then back to the unfazed staff.

Godfrey smiled. "Wherever you wish."

"You will begin the greatest education of your life tomorrow. Today, become better acquainted with each other and do honor by my highest right: *eat, drink, and be merry!*" Godfrey finished to enthusiastic applause, a great portion of which came from the boy next to Emile. The greatest admiration shone in his eyes.

While the rest dug into their dinners, Emile made a beeline for their headmaster, who was already entrenched in a full plate of meats and a large chalice of something pungent and amber.

"... The *Clown and the Bard*? That's just an old rumor. Do you believe everything you hear?" Godfrey was saying loudly to the same boy who'd interrupted his speech, who stood first in line to address Godfrey and bore a confused look. The boy left, looking somewhat dejected.

"Excuse me, but there's been a mistake," Emile said formally, stepping up. Godfrey disengaged himself from a fresh lamb kabob and looked up at her, his face still betraying no sign of recognition.

"I caught the wrong train. I'm supposed to be at Alvarus Academy."

"Ah, Emile?" he asked.

"Yes."

"There's no mistake. You were reassigned here."

"Why?" she balked.

"Occasionally we take an Alvarius student when it is felt that they are better suited to our curriculum."

"Who decided – ?"

"Before you get into a panic, take a look at your schedule!
You won't have classes like *these* at Alvarus."

Godfrey handed her a piece of paper from his pocket and
she read:

SKOLA LOM
YEARLY CURRICULUM

BODY LANGUAGE

STEALING

DRIVING DOWN DANGEROUS ROADS

LYING AND MANIPULATION

DRINKING

PROPER COOKING AND CLEANING

SENSUALITY

FOOLISHNESS

Godfrey was back to chewing his lamb as she digested
the information.

"Where are the real classes?" Emile asked.

Godfrey rent a booming laugh that evoked a shadow of the jester from at the bar.

"These classes will be more real to you than anything you've ever learned!"

"*'Body Language'*?" Emile repeated.

"You will learn to interpret and react instinctively to signals in your surrounding reality without hesitating or allowing yourself to be swayed by delusions and fantasies in your own head," Godfrey replied in a scholarly manner.

"But when will I learn math?" asked Emile.

"If you pay close enough attention to *Lying and Manipulation*, you will learn *when* to use math, as well as how to find those who know the math you need," he answered.

"But what about the math itself?" asked Emile.

"We do not teach the math itself."

Emile returned to her seat, suspecting the entire day for a practical joke. If it was, it was a highly elaborate one; none of the other students seemed to find anything unusual about their classes. The entire table was awash in frantic discussion over strategies and possible pitfalls.

"*'Driving Down Dangerous Roads'*? I don't know how to drive down *safe* roads!" Jesa fretted to Lillian.

"None of us are of age," Emile said.

"Already finding problems with something, Locronan?" her neighbor asked her.

"This *can't* be our real schedule," Emile said.

"Nervous?" he grinned."I'm not. I mastered all these classes years ago."

"Even 'Sensuality'?" asked a girl on his other side.

"*Especially* 'Sensuality'. And I'm happy to offer my superior tutoring services to any struggling ladies for free. At reduced cost," he said as an afterthought.

Emile resisted the urge to voice her doubt that he would pass a math class, had there been one.

Deep into dinner, a sudden drop in volume made some of the students, buried in their meals, glance around for the source of lack and see that the end of the table was empty save for a few staff, sitting quietly by themselves or chatting with the nearest student. Godfrey himself and the two on his either side had disappeared and the hall seemed to glow dimmer, as if a light had gone out.

"Does anyone know where Godfrey went?" asked the boy full of questions, who'd joined them at their seats and introduced himself as Barton. He'd been telling Emile for the past twenty minutes about his classroom woes and emerged from his own monologue more confused than he'd been going in.

"Probably to bed," said the dirty blonde boy with a straight face.

"You think so? It's pretty early," said Barton naively.

"You never know with Godfrey," Lillian dismissed, but she noted Godfrey's absence and began making motions to depart. Jesa gathered along with her and, right then, small pockets of the table rose up like bubbles: the beginnings of a slow trickle of all out of the hall.

"I've grown up hearing legends about Godfrey," Lillian said as Emile followed her and Jesa to the dorm rooms. The dirty blonde boy, his newest friend, and Barton walked behind them near enough to hear.

"Pretty much nobody in town knows him except the other teachers here."

"Godfrey seems like he'd make himself known wherever he went," said the blonde boy's friend.

"He's hard to catch. My father's only met him a few times and we've been here ten years!" Lillian turned back.

"Your dad's friends with Godfrey?" asked the dirty blonde.

"More like acquaintances."

"You must've heard good stories, then," he said.

"*Oh* yes."

"Everyone who lives here hears stories," Jesa added. "It's why they all want to come here."

"I have to get my luggage!" Emile remembered. "Will you wait for me?"

"We'll do better," Lillian said. She and Jesa veered away from the crowd with her into the quiet corner where Emile's bag waited, bypassing their fellows.

Lillian seemed pleased to see the boys' retreating backs as they continued down the hall with the rest. "That blonde one... he's good. Did you see that?"

Jesa nodded. "He sat right in the middle of all the girls."

"He's good," Lillian repeated. "He's one to watch out for."

"What do you mean, 'watch out for'?" Emile asked.

Her friends looked at each other.

"He'll be at the top in class," Lillian said.

Emile snorted. "He seemed like all talk."

"He's a showman but I don't think he was lying. And he'll try to get into Godfrey's good graces," Lillian said to Jesa's nod.

"I've met Godfrey before," Emile admitted. Lillian's eyes whipped onto her.

"You did? Where?"

"At a bar. He was there with all of the other teachers. The man and woman sitting around him – I saw them there, too."

"*You've* been to The Clown and the Bard?" Lillian's mouth dropped.

"I heard Godfrey say that was just a rumor."

"Well of course that's what he'd say, and yeah, the rumor is that's the bar where he goes. That's probably where he is now!" Lillian said. "You were there! It *is* real! What was it like?" her eyes burned with curiosity.

"It's filled with noisy drunks acting like animals. I thought Godfrey was homeless when I met him. What's the big deal?" Emile asked to their impressed faces.

"No one knows where it is or even what it looks like. Did you have a drink with them?"

"One," Emile remembered the encounter embarrassingly.

"What kind?"

"I'm not sure, it was green."

Lillian's face contorted into a mask of painful envy.

"Well? What happened?" she pressed. "Tell us

everything."

"I... I got lost, and Godfrey asked me what I was doing there, and what kind of person I was – I didn't know how to answer – he was too drunk, I don't think he even remembers me. Then I didn't say the right thing, and one of the men there pulled me out. And that's it. I don't remember it well myself. I was just trying to get home."

Lillian and Jesa looked at each other.

"How did you find it?" Lillian asked.

"I got lost one night and stumbled in.... But I don't know how."

"Do you remember what the sign looked like?" asked Lillian.

"There wasn't one."

Their eyes grew hungrier and their resolve appeared set, but they said nothing more of it as they walked the dark hall to the room, their conversation turning instead to what awaited them the next morning.

"A good, square meal to help you all start your day," one of the cooks said in the dining room the next morning. The beautiful breakfast buffet and the fresh spring morning through the open doors put Emile at ease among her fellows, where spirits were high and jokes about *Sensuality* rang so abundantly the subject no longer intimidated her. It seemed to put the bar out of Lillian's mind and she, too, was far calmer with them, pouring seconds of coffee for Jesa, Emile, and the others around them.

A few extra minutes to sit back and digest, letting the sounds of their voices wash around her like paints, and Emile caught the clock across the hall and jolted, getting a start on putting away her plates.

But when she returned to their table, Lillian and Jesa were nowhere in sight. She caught a few legs and arms turning down a hallway across the room and ran to catch up, walking into *Stealing* last and taking a seat in the last empty chair, next to the blonde boy from dinner.

"Morning, Locronan," he greeted her.

"I don't like that nickname," she responded.

"Sorry, Emile."

"It's fine."

"You're not even going to ask me my name? That's rude," he said.

"What's your name?" she asked reluctantly.

"Dorian," he offered her his hand to shake and when she did with his free hand he quickly grabbed the pen lying on her desk.

"Wh – I need that!" said Emile.

"Too bad. This is Stealing. It's nothing personal, I'm just getting a few extra points in," he said matter-of-factly before turning around.

"I don't care. I have more," she said coolly.

"Good thing this isn't Lying and Manipulation or you'd fail that, too."

"Everyone, hold up something of your neighbor's!" yelled a large middle aged man immediately as he walked through the door and up to the front of the room. With a kick to the stomach, Emile recognized him as the man who'd stood between her and Godfrey, who'd taken her beer and hoisted her out of the bar.

Most of her classmates were holding small objects they had stolen from their neighbors. Only she and a few other dumbfounded students came up empty handed, including Barton.

"Impressive! A hundred percent for today to everyone holding something up. The rest, zero."

A zero? In all of her years, she had never failed so much

as an assignment! She was a model student, the best in her class! Now, here, she was starting off with a zero?

"I am Gunter and I will be teaching you Stealing, one of life's most important trades. You win by taking, not by asking. Anyone who has taught you otherwise has taught you wrong."

Emile's stomach sank further.

"Stealing is an instinct. It does not debate. This is what you must hone to do well in my class. Some of you are more in touch. Others," his eyes passed over Emile, "will require more practice. But – let's see how forward thinking you are – what, can anyone tell me, is the *true* lesson of stealing?" he looked around the room.

"You can only rely on yourself to get what you want," Dorian replied and raised his hand in retrospect.

"*Yes. Double* points for this young man."

Dorian glowed with pride.

"You will be graded here both on how well you steal from others and how well you avoid being stolen from...."

Gunter's words filled Emile with dread. Her whole life she'd been taught not to steal, and now to pass she needed to do the opposite. How was she to go against everything that had been ingrained in her?

But Gunter spoke no more, switching to a passive role at the front of the class and offering no further direction. Slowly, chatter broke out among them again. Emile kept a guarded watch on her possessions for the rest of the class and ever scanned her peers, but when Dorian's fidget in her peripheral vision sent her arms flying over her desk in defense, he laughed. He appeared greatly at ease and his arms hung freely at his sides.

"Not a bad strategy," he nodded approvingly to her slowly roving eyes.

"Are you the teacher now?" she asked.

"Jeez, it's a compliment," he raised his hands, and, hesitating for a full half second, Emile made an ungainly grab as if moving through water for one of the many small objects that lay on his desk. It clattered onto the floor out of her palm and he snatched it up quickly.

He shrugged. "I don't care if you steal any of those. You can even have one," with a smile he handed her the eraser she'd been after. Meanwhile, the boy he'd made friends with the evening before grabbed a few bits of paper off of Dorian's desk, but he seemed unfazed.

"I didn't steal anything," Emile said to Jesa as they packed up at the end of the class.

"Don't worry. People are taking this way too seriously. It's the first day!"

Her words were balm. But as she went to put away her things, Emile realized she had nothing left – everything of hers had been stolen. She didn't know how. The only theft she saw was of Dorian and her pen.

"I don't even know *how* to steal. My parents never taught me," Emile complained.

"Don't worry, you'll learn," said Lillian, whom Emile saw was carrying a small pile of knick-knacks new to her.

"How many people did you steal from?" Dorian asked her.

"Five," Lillian said neutrally.

"I don't want to steal from others. I don't like it," said Emile as they climbed up a staircase behind others to Sensuality. "Do you?"

"It's what we have to if we want to pass," said Jesa.

"*We* don't have to steal from each other. We can make a pact," said Lillian to the two of them. "We can watch out for each other."

Emile readily agreed, warmed by the promise of safety.

But this newfound warmth dissipated upon her first

steps into the dimly lit, quiet *Sensuality* classroom and the same dread filled her again. The three of them wove among low cushioned chairs clustered around small round tables, bypassing deeply colored, intricate rugs adorning the stone walls. They took a table near the back near to where Dorian and his newly built crew sat attempting to hide their nerves.

From behind a set of embroidered crimson curtains draped over an alcove emerged the beautiful brunette lady, as seductive and regal as ever. She was Godfrey's counterpart, her presence filling every inch of the room, but instead of his bold, brazen air, hers was soft, feminine, luxuriant. It swam through their senses like heavy perfume.

"I suspect this is the first exposure to *Sensuality* for all of you," she began invitingly. The table of Dorian, the friend who had stolen from him – a spiky haired boy named Max – and, to their clear displeasure, Barton, maintained stoic expressions along with the rest, while the less tough looked shyly down at their tables. Their teacher introduced herself as Jacqueline .

"This class will unlock worlds for you. What you learn here you will never be able to unlearn. Like any class, Sensuality is an art, and to succeed you must possess artifice." Her technical take fell out of sync with her warm manner. "Mastering the techniques of Sensuality will reveal to you many what I suspect will be painful truths. I expect – and so should you – that this will be your most shattering class, for Sensuality touches a part of us that we have little control over."

With a single glance Jacqueline conveyed the dispassionate calculators each of them would become in the realm of attraction, her sparkling eyes tunnels letting them glimpse at their ends the disillusionment by experience none of them could escape, just as she had not. Emile averted them when they fell on her; their gaze was too intense, too scanning, too knowing. She did not want to believe what it said.

"We will begin today with appearance, a consideration you should maintain always going forward in your lives. No more do you have the luxury of ignorance. I lift the veil off of you forever.... Sensuality starts with the visual. But, despite all you learn today, make no mistake; that is only the very beginning...."

Jacqueline taught the girls tricks to mature their appearance, and she taught the boys how to enjoy them. While the girls styled their hair and adjusted their expressions, the boys beheld, were swayed by one detail over another, opened their pores wider to let the intoxicating perfume in.

"These skills are the essence of womanhood," Jacqueline said later, words that fell into Emile's stomach as she followed each motion hesitantly. An image of her simple, clear-faced mother stood beside the haughty, gilded Jacqueline who looked down at them from her high cheekboned face. Emile's mother wore her hair in a simple bun. Her cool cotton dress was practical and comfortable. She did not engineer herself towards beauty, yet it flowed out her in gentle waves; not in the vibrancy Jacqueline gushed like an irrepressible fountain, but like a calm, misty sea. Was it not enough? Did her mother's simple demeanor lack a pull? If her father saw Jacqueline, would he fall under her spell and forget about her mother? Emile didn't want to think about it. She didn't want to visualize the thoughts that crowded her mind like worms spewing up from that fountain.

She plaited her hair quietly beside Lillian and Jesa, who seemed to be going along fine. Jacqueline glided over to them and Lillian quickly tensed up, taking extra care to make her plait as neat as possible and to look especially seductive while at the task.

Jacqueline placed her arms on her shoulders and adjusted her position like a mannequin's.

"Pay mind to your angles," Jacuqeline said as she did.

"You must not only consider your static appearance; more important is movement, and you must always maintain an awareness of how you move and how it is seen."

Jesa had paused to lean back and watch Jacqueline's tutelage, her shoulder blades balancing her tosro against her chair and her arms folded neatly while her long plait draped over one of them.

"Effortless," Jaqueline said to her. "Did you girls consider tinting your lips? A subtle hint of color goes a very long way... but don't be afraid to be bold as well," Jacqueline glanced at a chest of drawers behind the curtain that was full of shimmering, sparkling odds.

"Emile! Grab some before the others do! Our hands are tied," said Lillian while Jesa adjusted her plait with care and Jacqueline watched them dispassionately.

"Get the best ones," Lillian called in a hiss as Emile walked over.

The chest against the wall was old and peeling, made of solid dark wood and covered in one of the intricate drapes that adorned the wall, manifesting perfect synchronicity with the classroom. The small top drawer she found filled with a rainbow of lipsticks and eyeshadows, a logger's store of dark pencils and brushes, a well stocked pantry of glittery, shimmery pots. The drawer below overflowed with fabrics satin and glittery, pinks and fuchsias, reds and violets, trailing ribbons, vests and boas, shawls, hats, and simply swaths of fabric. Emile grabbed several bags of makeup and as much fabric as her arms could carry to bring to the table.

Jesa and Lillian dove in, lacing shimmery ribbons into each other's hair and draping each other with shawls and laughter.

"No no, that color's too bold for your baby face," said Lillian, snatching a tube of rich red lipstick from Emile's hand. "It's more for someone with my coloring. Try this one," she handed her a baby pink lipstick.

"Here," Jesa took the tube into her expert hand and applied it to Emile's lips. "Oh that looks *so* cute on you!" she stood back to examine and held up a mirror. Emile studied her reflection. The plastic pink hue contrasted garishly with her peach cheeks, and the unaccustomed plait hung awkwardly around her neck.

Emile looked around at the rest of the class laughing and playing dress up. She caught the first of gazes fired through the feathers and glitter thickly obscuring the air, and could see the beginnings of a web of connections forming around her that would grow stronger and deeper into the year.

These trifles mean nothing! Emile cried to herself, turning back to her falsified reflection in despair. Would boas and glitter be the determiners of some of the most important outcomes in her life? It couldn't be so. Even more so than *Stealing*, the lessons of *Sensuality* went against the rules directing her from within.

"Is everything alright, Emile?" Jacqueline noted her unease.

"I feel artificial," said Emile.

"Good. You must. Sensuality is artifice," said Jacqueline.

"But what place does artifice have in love?" asked Emile.

It was as if spoken in a foreign language. Movements stopped. Rustling beads stilled around the room Heads perked up and spun onto her.

Jacqueline looked coldly down from her height, and for a second Emile saw a stir in a subterranean pool sitting long still under the layered mists of those eyes.

"Fifty point deduction," she said.

"But I don't understand," Emile cried. "I thought that in love you're supposed to be your freest self. Am I wrong? I can see your beauty, plainly, and all of the experiences that stand behind it shine through your movements. They tell a story, but it goes against what my own heart says. And if what you say from a lifetime of experience is true, then why does my heart tell me otherwise?" Emile could not contain the conflict.

After a pause, Jacqueline replied, "I only teach the subject matter I understand," before dismissing their class.

Emile headed to *Lying and Manipulation* with the irresolute clashing between her past and what she had learned today in *Sensuality* still churning inside her.

"Here," a woman curtly handed Emile a slip of paper. Emile recognized immediately the snippy blonde who had been sitting at the bar with Jacqueline and who had taken to Emile even less than had Gunter.

'Windows,' read Emile's paper. Emile looked up at the enormous stained glass windows on the wall.

Their teacher made no comment on switching *Lying and Manipulation* with *Proper Cooking and Cleaning*, and many started on their chores. Eager to pass at least one class, Emile followed suit. It was easy, straightforward work; she didn't have to focus on the others. While ruminating on this she nearly tripped over Dorian sitting on the floor with his legs out, leaning against the wall and eating an apple.

"You're done already?" Emile asked.

"My buddy Barton and I thought it would be more

efficient if we combined our chores. He had dishes and I had counters," Dorian said easily.

Emile glanced over at Barton, furiously washing that morning's mountain of dirty breakfast dishes in the huge sink basin, with all of the dusty trinkets Dorian had gathered off of the counter tops in a pile beside the sink, awaiting their turn.

"So you're just letting him do all the work?" Emile demanded.

"I did my part! The counters have never looked better," he said and took another bite of his apple. "That's what I'm putting on the write-up, anyway."

"Your loss. You'll fail Proper Cooking and Cleaning," said Emile.

"*Au contraire*, I'm saving my strength for Cooking and Cleaning this afternoon."

"This afternoon? Wh – ?"

"I'll let you in on a little secret," he said, beckoning her forward. "This is Lying and Manipulation, Emile. It just *looks* like Proper Cooking and Cleaning. You can ask Betsy if you don't believe me, but I'd wait until after class to get the truth."

At once Emile stopped and looked around the classroom.

Most of their classmates were hard at work scrubbing floors, dusting corners, and polishing silverware, but a few stood conspicuously off to the side, and nobody who was wholly absorbed in their chores noticed the ones who hadn't raised a finger all class.

Just as the realization crashed over her and she dropped her rag, Betsy returned with their scores.

Dorian glowed with his hundred while Emile tucked away yet another zero.

They ate lunch on newly cleaned dishes and went to *Proper Cooking and Cleaning,* where they washed them all over again and where Emile found herself worn out from her scrupulous cleaning efforts in *Lying and Manipulation,* angrily watching Dorian scrub the floors with single-minded focus before she nearly drove herself and Lillian off a cliff in an old car in *Driving Down Dangerous Roads.*

She trundled with the rest to their last class, *Foolishness,* at the top of the old castle tower. An unspoken sentiment ran through the students. They understood the usefulness of *Lying and Manipulation,* of *Stealing,* of *Cooking and Cleaning,* and of *Sensuality* – but what use *Foolishness* would be to them not one could see. Dorian openly sneered at the class along the way, but stopped immediately when he saw that their teacher was Godfrey.

They had not seen him all day. Presently he sat behind a simple desk in the plain, comfortable classroom. On the shelf behind him sat his jester's hat like a trophy, its floppy arms hanging calm and limp.

"Welcome to Foolishness, your last class but your most important one," he began. "It is an easy class, but in spite of this, most of you will fail," he paused. "In order to pass you must understand only one thing: it is fine to be a fool."

"Why is Foolishness more important than Lying and Manipulation?" Dorian asked, shocking all with his voluntary question except Lillian, who shot Jesa and Emile a knowing, if somewhat self-satisfied, look.

"Because if you don't also learn to be a Fool, the skills you master will master you," answered Godfrey. "Do you know what Foolishness is?"

Dorian shrugged, "Being an idiot?"

"No. There are plenty of idiots without a trace of Foolishness. In fact, they are idiots *because* they are not Foolish. Foolishness is simply the sense to not take yourself seriously. It is the act of sacrificing your pride, which the world will tell you is, well, foolish. After all, pride moves you forward and up. I can see that none of you are Fools," Godfrey continued, looking around. "However, you need only to pass once in order to pass the class, so don't worry. Fools never worry!"

He dismissed them.

"I don't understand Foolishness at all," Lillian muttered as they walked back to their rooms.

"I don't understand *any* of the classes," Emile lamented.

"You'll improve," Jesa comforted. "It's probably just first day shock. I think we're all overwhelmed."

To this even Dorian didn't let out a snide remark.

For the rest of the week nobody made progress in *Foolishness,* not even Dorian and Lillian, who rapidly rose to the top of every class. Emile, meanwhile, did not improve in any. She perceived herself swimming through Lom upstream, moving against the others who seemed free of tangles to undo before absorbing the lesson of the day. And whatever she thought she learned came quickly undone. At the slightest gain of a firm foothold, the rug was pulled out from under her, whether by Max stealing her supplies in *Proper Cooking and Cleaning* to earn points for *Stealing*, or Lillian's makeover on her in *Sensuality* earning her a zero while Emile's careful, expert job gained Lillian top points. The teachers never tested on what they said they were testing; the true test was always something else. A revelation for hindsight, and never spoken out loud. Who could she ask, fallen far behind the pack? Lillian and Jesa mastered every lesson with ease. From the second night forth, Emile couldn't keep up with the conversations on classroom dynamics and tactics that broke out during dinner.

She separated quietly from the rest after the week's last *Foolishness* lesson, her mind an unraveled spool and her heart wrung out ten times a day, skipping dinner and heading to their empty room to take refuge on her bed. Lillian and Jesa were down there getting a head start on the next week, no doubt, and Emile would fall further behind once more Yet who was keeping her apart now? Nobody's hand but her own! What did she herself think of their pact to watch out for one another?

It was this realization that moved her off her bed and, with renewed hope, pushed Emile to seek out Lillian, Jesa, and the others at dinner. The halls were empty and as dark by now as if the house was asleep. Only the absence of clanking dishes hinted at how many hours had passed in her reverie. The only sound breaking the peace came from mumbling voices around a corner as she approached the end of the hall.

"...Barton," a voice that was surely Lillian's muttered matter-of-factly.

"Doormat," responded Dorian in the same tone.

"He *loves* you."

"Yeah. When he sat with us that first day, we were ready to destroy him in Sensuality, but then we realized, he's the perfect third," Dorian said while Max's chuckle came in.

"Does whatever we tell him," said Max.

"I think know what you mean," Lillian said to a new wave of surreptitious laughs.

"So innocent," entered Jesa's voice. "She didn't even realize I stole all her things the first day of Stealing."

"How did she end *up* here?" asked Max.

"I don't know but I give her a week. Between Emile and Barton, who d' you think's the more hopeless?" Dorian asked.

"Oh, Emile has a major leg up," Lillian said.

"Really," Dorian replied, and a lowered tone seemed to indicate that the group drew closer together.

"Emile has actually *been* to the Clown and the Bard," Lillian said, her voice hushed but urgent, as if she had been waiting for the entire conversation to divulge this.

"*How?*" asked Max.

"She said she got lost and stumbled in."

"Sounds about right," said Dorian flatly.

"She's the only one who would recognize it. I know *about* where it is, but I have no idea what it looks like. And it's sure to be hidden," said Lillian.

"Do you know what this means? She's our only hope for Drinking. *Emile* is our only hope for *Drinking*," said Dorian. "Either that or she's killing Lying and Manipulation."

"Emile doesn't lie," said Jesa.

"You better stay in her good books," Dorian said.

"We're best friends," Lillian assured.

Tears in her eyes, Emile turned rapidly around to the dying chuckles. Was this her first taste of *Foolishness?* How could she have been so naïve as to trust Lillian's reassurances of their friendship? She should have realized what her seat at the top of the class meant!

The nature of their predicament became clear at last as she fled down the hall. These teachers were not their mentors but fickle demigods, driven by their caprices and making rules that bent like the shadows of a flickering candle. Her peers *admired* Godfrey and Jacqueline; but *she* was the one out of her element, a country girl dropped into a lion's den. Max was hard but right; how *did* she come to be here? Betsy and Gunter had told her she didn't belong, and their sentiment hadn't changed by her coming to their school. It was Godfrey alone who had wondered if she wasn't one of them. Had she not stumbled into the bar, she would have never been transferred to Lom! And how had she, Emile, hovering at the bottom of the class, managed to find the secret that so eluded everybody else? It was that light, bobbing in and out of her moment of darkness held in a tiny hand. That light had been as flickering as anything in this world; after all, it was of this world. That *girl* was of this world! If the bar was here, she must be here, too. *She* would be able to explain this world to Emile, to tell her why she had fallen into a place where she didn't belong.

Holding her resolution close, she made her way to the main hall where in the moonlight falling through its ceiling high windows the grand wooden entrance stood unmanned.

"Going for a stroll?" a n amused voice asked behind her as she reached within feet of the door.

Godfrey was framed in a peripheral archway, calmly observing her catlike tread.

Emile's heart jumped; the last thing she wanted was Godfrey privy to her plans.

"I'm sending a letter to my parents," she thought quickly. "I'm going to the post office."

"Students are not allowed out after dark. A teacher is

standing guard by the door at all times," he said.

"Then when can I send them a letter?"

"You must not have heard when I went over our complete isolation policy. We believe our students need total severance of ties to the outside world to properly learn our material," Godfrey stated.

"Do you mean that I *can't* write to my parents?"

"Parents, uncles, friends, paramours... anyone on the outside."

"What if they write me? How will I get their letters?"

"They won't. You won't."

"That can't be true!" she cried.

"It is part of the value of our degree," Godfrey said in the same earnest tone he had used to explain *Body Language*.

He knew, she thought. He must have sensed the gist of her intent to escape. Without a word she headed back in the direction of her room. But she couldn't return. Not if it meant sitting before Lillian and Jesa's calculated sustainments at friendship. She was isolated within the school and now she was isolated from the world beyond its walls. With the desperation of a cornered animal, Emile turned down an unfamiliar hall, moving as far away from Godfrey as possible and walking into a carpeted hallway out of use in their classes. No signs of life stirred here, and Emile realized just how much empty space there must be throughout their school. Even if she got expelled, she could probably find somewhere to hide.

Emile hadn't a clue of anyone's whereabouts, except, ironically, Godfrey's, the last creature she wanted to see. This – it struck like a bolt in the midst of her fuming march – was useful information. Another exit had to lay somewhere and in these distant recesses it could be unmanned. Seeing the promise of moonlight through windows at the far end again, she carefully tested passing doors until one near the end of the hall yielded .

Her explorations had led her into a magnificent library. It was a hallowed and far removed sanctum that felt seldom used but must have once been a cherished, frequented space, too ornately was it furnished with the kinds of Persian rugs and wall hangings that hung in their classrooms to be a mere storage space. Its rows of dusty shelves were full of books appearing to be thick collections of encyclopedias or the like. She followed them down to their end at the rough stone wall, illuminated softly by light falling through the windows from the wall adjacent at the castle's quieter end.

It was in the darkest corner of the room that she saw it

by a ripple in a rug: blending into the floorboards to near invisibility was a little doorway, easily assumed for the entrance to a crawl space except for a distinctive marking by the wall's edge of a crude lamp containing a star. It was faint, but when she traced the etching with her finger, she grew sure of the mark's shape. She withdrew in disbelief. It was the mark of the wanderer!

Emile wedged her fingernails into the crevices and lifted the door easily along a well masked hinge with a low creak. There was just enough light throughout the library to illuminate the first two steps of a rough stone staircase before it dropped into a pool of darkness. Emile stepped down cautiously into a pool of cold air. Pressing her hands against the stairwell, she slowly sank further in until her head was just below the hatch, then reached up and pulled the rug, folding and jamming it underneath to supply the merest light when she lowered the hatch softly upon it.

She descended a few more steps into not a room but a low, narrow tunnel of stone and earth not the width of her wingspan.

The tunnel extended beyond the weak overhead light into darkness once more. The weightless veil of pitch black blindness pressed softly on her from all sides as she went forth with the path's curvature, going faster as she gained surety and adjusted to sightless navigation. The first step down took her by surprise, but was a promising sign that the tunnel was moving downhill into town. Emile slowed and moved carefully from then on, relying more on the air that grew colder, then warmer; by then she had walked at least twice the length of the castle, she guessed. Without warning a dim light filled the tunnel once more from the far end ahead,thrown upon the lumpy earthen walls turned peaty brown. Excitedly, Emile sped up toward escape and knocked into a rough wooded doorway almost the tunnel's height. There was an inch-high gap between the wood and the earthen floor, and carved all the way through the doorway in the top, like a large eyehole, was the star-bearing lamp. The light came in through these openings. Emile pressed her eye to it. She had found the wanderer's home! She had found where the light had disappeared to!

She could make out nothing. No hints of furniture, no detail of any kind; only a sea of dim light from no point source. She knocked softly. After a minute of silence she knocked again, harder. Pressing her ear, she heard only the utter silence of the underground, yet she sensed life pulsing like a heartbeat on the other side. Emile pounded, crying "open!", but not even a footstep came near. The door stayed stubbornly shut. After many more futile attempts, Emile turned around. *It's late now. I'll try again,* she explained to herself as she retraced the tunnel back to the castle, climbing uncomfortably uphill this time up to the library and the much dimmer pool of light she herself had cast still there to light her way up. The hatch and the rug lay untouched to her relief, but to her horror the library was no longer silent.

"...That's the secret! They're not just testing us during class, they're testing us all the time!" a familiar voice sent her heart pounding when she pushed the little door up. She could barely make out the frantic words muffled by a sound barrier.

"We can get points for Stealing in any of the other classes, so why would it stop at the end of the day? That's why we don't know which rules are really rules and which they want us to break – " Lillian addressed an audience emphatically.

"What was that?" Dorian's voice cut in sharply. Emile froze. The hatch had creaked. She waited for them to resume talking before pushing it just a bit more to squeeze herself out, hop lightly up, and smooth the rug over the hatch in the swiftest execution of motions she had ever carried out.

"They *want* us to find it. How else are we going to pass Drinking? Otherwise it has to be one of the classes we fail!"

Sudden footsteps rounded the row and Dorian's

triumphant face appeared at the edge of the shelves.

"Reading?" he smiled as Lillian, Jesa, Max, and Barton came around after him.

Emile had neither light nor book. "Looking for something to read," she said.

"Right."

"Just like you?" she countered, determinedly ignoring the hatch to her left.

The group quickly exchanged looks and seemed to wordlessly reach a consensus.

"We're figuring out how to pass Drinking," Dorian said, and she could tell he wasn't lying. "I don't know if you noticed, but we haven't had a single class and we're all failing."

"I noticed that," she said, unconsciously leaning back from the poorly contained anticipation buzzing about five faces. It hit her that they had hoped to find her here, the veteran barfly, and that Dorian had taken the lead in playing it cool.

"Well, they're all drunks. They must have some liquor lying around. A library's a good place to hide things, no?" Dorian said.

"Plus, the front door is blocked," added Barton, oblivious to the irritation at his off timing of information. "A couple kids got caught sneaking out through there earlier this week and got zeros."

"I know, I ran into Godfrey on guard there earlier tonight," said Emile.

"Wait. *You're* trying to do the same thing, aren't you!" Dorian's face brightened with revelation. "You're trying to sneak out!"

Emile froze, caught off her guard.

Dorian rolled his eyes. "Come on, we all know you've been to the Clown and the Bard. We can help each other. We can help you leave the school and you can help us find the bar. We came here looking for you. I figured after a week of class you could only be at the library, and I was right."

They looked at her expectantly now that the truth was revealed.

"Does everyone know about that?" asked Emile.

"Just us," said Lillian.

"You think we're idiots? They'd try to recruit you," said Dorian.

"But I don't know how to get there."

"I do," Lillian said quickly. "And you know what it looks like. Between the two of us we can find it."

"Except you're forgetting that we're stuck in the castle," Barton reminded them.

"There's no way out here. I've been looking since dinner," Emile added, a bit too quickly for her liking.

"You said Godfrey was standing guard?" asked Max slowly.

"That was an hour ago."

Lillian gave a sudden laugh of triumph. "He was probably sneaking off to the bar himself!"

"It *is* Friday night," Jesa said.

"Then someone else is on guard," said Barton.

"Who?" asked Max. "It's dead."

"Not Godfrey, I'll tell you that much," said Dorian.

"Gaunt?" Max proposed.

"Gaunt is more likely to guard the bar itself. That's what he did when I was there," said Emile.

"Jacqueline?" asked Barton. Jesa and Lillian laughed, and even Emile chuckled.

"Like she or Betsy would get left behind," said Lillian.

"Gunter?" Barton went down the list. All of them ruled out Gunter immediately.

"Maybe it's one of the cooks," Barton said.

"I'll take my chances with them," said Dorian.

"Maybe it's no one. Maybe it's another of Godfrey's tricks!" it hit Emile. She vaguely recalled seeing their entire cadre of teachers on that night at the bar.

"Could be," Dorian said, taken aback.

"Then what are we dicking around for," said Max, and they hurried to the main hall.

"You really want to risk this?" Barton whispered as they ran. Dorian stopped.

"Well, I don't know. It'd definitely be easier just to find something to drink here," he mused.

"It'd be even better if we found another exit," Jesa said.

"I'll risk it," said Lillian. "And we need Emile if we sneak out. She and I can go."

"Max and I can look for another exit, meanwhile," Jesa said.

"I guess you and I are hunting for booze," Dorian put his arm around Barton. "If you get the back of the house, I'll do the front."

"Sure," Barton said with solidarity.

"Alright. Let's break."

Dorian split off for the front and Barton went back toward the library.

"You said you didn't find any doors back here?" Jesa asked Emile.

"No."

"Then we'll head back," she and Max followed Lillian and Emile to the entrance, Dorian already far ahead of them.

"No guard! We're free!" Dorian ran back from the front to meet them a minute later.

"Brilliant, Emile," whispered Lillian as they bounded for the door and she grabbed her hand.

"Shouldn't we get Barton?" Emile asked.

"If we go back for him, there might be someone here by the time we return," Jesa said. "We have to take the chance."

They ran down the steps and out the gate, celebrating their luck and craft. For the first time she gazed at the town in the night. Pale beige and brown shone out beneath the muted brick red roofs, lights strung all around the network of winding cobblestone roads and people moving out and about in pairs or small groups telling them it was no quiet night.

Many looked at them curiously. They were by far the youngest. If they ran into any of the teachers there would be no way to hide. While the others planned their strategies for *Drinking,* Emile looked around for a little nimble figure or a flickering lamp. Lillian seemed to know exactly where she was going.

"See it yet?" Lillian asked. Emile was sure she had been down none of the streets they'd traversed and shook her head.

"Pay attention. It's somewhere here, I know," Lillian said. Her next turn brought them onto a street Emile recognized immediately. Surprising herself, she spotted the old recessed building without effort, its worn oak door unmistakable for any other now that she knew how to find it and the same dark curtains hanging on its little window.

"That one," she stopped and stood before it.

"This? This doesn't even look open. Or like a bar," said Dorian. "Where's the sign?"

"There isn't one," Lillian recalled. "You're sure it's this?" she seemed doubtful.

"As sure as I'll be."

"After you, then," Max nudged her forward, hanging behind in fear with the rest, waiting to see what would happen.

Emile pushed the door and stepped into a familiar dim space, crowded with people including several of their teachers sprinkled in. The rest followed Emile and shut the door behind them. No one paid them any notice.

For the briefest moment, Emile caught, as if suspended in a moment out of time, Dorian scanning the scene beside her before settling on an action and, before anyone else could perceive it, snapping on his usual enthusiasm to boldly lead their way ahead.

"Well look who's back!" cried the bushy bearded bartender who had served her months ago when they were several feet from the bar. Emboldened and slightly stunned, Emile led the way to the bar and she and the rest took up stools.

"Same as last time?" he smiled through the hairy tangle, looking over them all.

"No, thank you," Emile said. "You remember me?" she asked nervously.

He laughed. "Of course I remember you!" He brought out a round of shot glasses filled with honey hued liquid.

"On the house!" he smiled at the crowd of them, introducing himself as Brody.

Dorian threw Emile a raised glance and a grin. The four of them toasted like naturals and Emile hesitantly followed suit, downing the liquid in one gulp a second behind. It tasted as sweet as it looked.

"How is it?" Brody asked as Emile straightened her face.

"Good," she said to his laugh.

"Students sneaking in, huh? Your secret's safe with me," he grinned.

"You served us," Lillian pointed out.

"I was a student once. I know what you have to do."

Jesa grew immediately interested, and Brody, leaning over the bar that separated him from the rest of the room, answered all of her and Lillian's eager questions about Lom with a new round of drinks until Jesa asked him about the mysterious green one he'd made Emile last time and Brody explained the mechanics to her in great detail as he made her her own.

Emile sat back for a moment, getting her bearings. Lillian, she noticed, was doing the same. None of them other than Jesa spoke for a long moment, merely nursing their drinks and watching the crowd. Was this what they came here for, Emile wondered. She saw Lillian glance at Jesa every now and read something like jealousy on her face.

"Told you Jacqueline and Betsy wouldn't miss out!" Lillian said suddenly as a small mass of bodies shifted away from the center of the floor and Jacqueline, Betsy, and two other women came into view around a table, glittering under candlelight in satin and shimmering shawls.

Lillian jumped off her stool, seizing the chance to slip into the circle and smoothly catching Jesa's eye. Jesa procured her green drink from Brody and followed. Max, observing these motions, quickly joined along and the three of them made their way to the table, catching a stunned but clearly amused Jacqueline off guard.

Dorian hung back and watched, reclining easily against the bar, sunk so deeply into the warm ochre walls as if painted right into the scene of warm-toned glasses and bawdy drunken characters, which Emile perched on her stool uneasily just outside of.

"Too soon," he said, shaking his head. "I'm taking my time with Drinking first," he finished the one in his hand. "That your game plan?" he turned to Emile casually.

"I'm done drinking."

"But you'll fail the class!" he gave her an incredulous look.

"I don't care. Why would I want a certificate that proves I can lie and manipulate people?"

Dorian chuckled. "I bet when someone in your village wanted something, they said it. I bet when someone offered to help their neighbors, their neighbors said thank you and left it at that. I bet it was all so simple and straightforward, that your mom never wanted to put on a corset and your dad never wanted another woman because they have a perfect marriage and they're so *nice.*"

"What's wrong with all that?" asked Emile.

"Nothing, I guess. Just seems boring."

"It wasn't boring for me," said Emile. "I could've stayed there forever."

"So why didn't you?"

"My parents moved us back to Prague. That's where I was born. We moved to Locronan when I was five."

"So *that's* it!" Dorian smiled widely as if he'd finally solved a riddle. "You have a grain of it in you."

"A grain of what?"

"We could call it curiosity. Your old life isn't enough for you."

"This life isn't for me," she waved around. "I can't keep up with the game."

"I'm only aware of the game because I *have* to be," Dorian

said. "Close your eyes for a second and it could be your head."

Some people see with their eyes open; some with their eyes closed, she remembered Godfrey's words. *Which are you?*

Dorian turned to her and said quietly. "You see their plan?" he glanced at Lillian, Jesa, and Max, continuing when she stayed silent. "Lillian and Jesa want points for Sensuality during Drinking, which is more points for crossing classes. Max is the only guy among a group of girls. Oldest trick in the book. Not a bad plan."

"So why didn't you go with them?"

"Didn't want to make their mistake. *They* went to the teachers. Nor terrible, but a little amateur. The teachers'll be here all night."

"I don't know how to see all that," said Emile. "I thought everyone was just here for Drinking."

"No one comes to the bar just to drink," Dorian said.

"I did!" said Emile. But she realized a moment later that this was a lie. It was her search for the wanderer that had brought her here, and everywhere she turned her head, she kept an eye out for that figure. The debauchery before her senses was white noise. Dorian was right. She wasn't simply here to drink. She wasn't here to drink at all. Did that make her one of them? Was that the grain?

"I know what your problem is. You need another one of these," he dangled her empty shot glass.

"I said I'm done."

"Come on, Emile. Drinking will help you with all the other classes," and he cried, "Bartender!" with such aplomb it sounded as if he'd been coming to the Clown and the Bard for years. But Emile would not forget that initial moment of fright when he paused, not yet Dorian, to get his bearings before donning a mask tailored perfectly to the situation.

"Brody, could we get another round?"

"Certainly."

Dorian, who'd been manipulating and leading her astray all week; Dorian, who was now sitting next to her sharing a drink like a friend; Emile felt silly beside his exaggerated sense of cool but toasted him nonetheless.

Godfrey's roar carried across the bar and they saw him on the other end, dancing like a fool in his jester's hat to jeers and cheers from a table full of drunken men. He was no longer the dirty bum but the headmaster dancing on the throne of this underground kingdom and its whole dark charade flowing out from his flailing limbs. He stomped on the ground like a two ton bear, rattling the glasses with every footfall. Beer sprayed from his audience's laughing mouths and fell in glistening droplets to the floor.

His unbridled freedom seized hold of Emile. His arms reached to the scuffed ceiling; he drank his current pint down in enormous gulps; he laughed from his belly until the laughter ran out, while Emile clung to the reef of herself in this chaotic candlelit ocean. She marveled at how easily he could he let himself go with such unbridled release in a world where everyone was ready to eat each other alive. But then, this was his domain. He was the king. He was himself inconsiderately.

From the middle table, Lillian and Jessica called to Dorian and Emile, urged on by Jacqueline and Betsy's eyes. Dorian jumped down instantly and stumbled over, heeding their beckon.

"Come on, Emile!" Lillian cried to the resistant Emile, who felt herself pulled in by obligation.

Jacqueline and Betsy were busy discussing the gossip of castle life – who was who's lover and what so-and-so's true motivations were were analyzed with the sharpest, most cunning deductions. Lillian listened raptly to every word of this hard scrutiny, burning to know for herself the ins and outs of the castle and gasping whenever someone's secret was revealed. She'd put on a velvety pink corset and a glittery shawl to match Jacqueline's while Jesa had donned a sultry black corset with red stripes. They fit right in at the table where moments ago they had been strangers too intimidated to enter the bar.

"We got you something, Emile," Jesa handed Emile a red corset with black lacy trimming. "Dorian needs to approve."

Emile flushed to near the corset's shade.

"No, thanks," she said.

"We're *helping*," said Lillian. "Do you wan to fail *all* the classes?"

"It's not for me," said Emile stiffly. Jacqueline's smug, silent expression told her she had already docked points from her next lesson.

"Rummage through these," Jacqueline said coolly, pulling a bag full of eccentric accessories from under the table. They were bright, feathered boas, glittery broad-rimmed hats, long lace gloves and plastic pipes. The remnants of a costume store crossed with an urban boutique. Emile recognized some of them from the large chest she'd scavenged through in their first *Sensuality* lesson. "They're yours to keep," Jacqueline added as Lillian pulled out a lurid fuchsia boa that looked like its first home had been a circus.

"This is points for Sensuality *and* Foolishness!" Lillian exclaimed, throwing it over her neck.

"I dare you wear that all night," said Jesa with relish.

"You wear this," she handed Jesa a wide-rimmed mesh hat topped with stale fake flowers and dusty ribbons that somehow complemented her corset.

A slightly blurry Godfrey stumbled to their table, far more reminiscent of the man Emile first met than of the headmaster of an institution.

"Don't have all the fun without me!" he cried, nearly shattering Emile's eardrum and wafting his putrid breath into her face.

"Looks like you're already dressed for the costume party," said Dorian to him. Emile barely made out a quaver in his bravado.

"Looks like the *hat's* out of the *bag!!*" Godfrey roared, receiving the attack with approval and slapping Dorian on the back. "This boy's ahead of the game! Preemptive Putdowns isn't until *weeks* from now!"

"And this one *here!*" his heavy arm fell over Emile.

"Don't we know it!" shouted Lillian.

"She won't drink, she won't tap into her sexuality – "

"I don't know *how* you expect to get your certificate, Emile," Lillian admonished.

"Here," Jesa took a ridiculous clown ruffled collar from the bag and rammed it over Emile's head where it choked her neck and stuffed dust up her nose. "At least you can get points for Foolishness."

Lillian and Jesa laughed, sitting among the queens and kings with their femininity enhanced while making of Emile the jester.

"That's points for Manipulation, right?" Lillian appealed to Godfrey and the other teachers anxiously.

"Brody!" Godfrey roared, throwing his head back to the bar. "Another round!"

Brody came through to their crowded table with a tray full of shot glasses, which Godfrey grandly passed around. Lillian and Dorian glowed with pride to be drinking with the headmaster himself, and even Emile, already tipsy, felt the wave brush her side. They all toasted together and slammed their glasses down.

Emile felt perfect. She had crossed a threshold onto a plateau where her movements flowed out with ease. Life was a party and everything she did was right, from the volume of her laughter to throwing her arms onto Dorian's shoulders when he returned from the bar with a beer. Her cognition lagged behind like a runner through water, affording only dim awareness at the time. She heard the stupid comments leaving her mouth and read his shocked expression and crooked grin a minute too late, after she'd slipped off her stool and instinctively ran toward the bar.

Brody had a glass of water waiting for her. She downed it.

"Where is the bathroom?" she asked and followed Brody's pointing finger to a door and down a shallow flight of steps, making it in just in time to throw up into the toilet bowl. She came up still smiling from where they'd broken off in the conversation before plunging down to vomit again.

"Are you okay, Emile?" she heard Brody's voice hazily through the locked bathroom door.

"I'm fine!" she called back, sitting up from the toilet bowl where the new contents swirled. She flushed it and remained on the floor, breathing, feeling better. Then she stood up and looked in the mirror. A slovenly face looked back at her with small, drunk eyes and hair that was a bird's nest with bits of vomit caked into the ends. Her forehead was beaded with sweat. Her mouth had uttered stupidities beyond anything she knew it could. What separated her now from the rest? She had forgotten about the wanderer and her light to roll around like a common animal, searching for nothing, content to bask in the swamp of gaudy costumes, games, and fleeting good feelings.

She stayed in the bathroom until she felt halfway normal again, throwing up more amid her head's swirling and panting. Once the door opened for a hand with a jug of water, which she drank to instant relief.

The bar was nearly empty when she reemerged. All of her classmates were gone and Godfrey was no longer roaring; he was passed out on a bench with a ragged blanket thrown over him, his beloved hat falling off of his sweaty head. Jacqueline and Betsy were nowhere to be seen.

"Where is everybody?" Emile asked, sitting at the bar where Brody cleaned glasses in the calm and kept an eye on the bar's last patrons.

"It cleared out. You were down there a while."

"What about Lillian?"

"They all left a while ago. Godfrey kicked them out. He can get fickle about the company in his bar."

"*His* bar?"

Brody nodded.

"I thought it was just his favorite. I didn't know he owned it."

"Since long before my time, and I've been here since I finished at Lom."

"So you're one of them, too," Emile groaned.

Brody smiled at her under his beard. "If it makes you feel better, I didn't get my certificate. But that's just between you and me."

"It does make me feel better," she admitted. "I don't understand. You fit in so perfectly," she said in wonderment.

"I did okay. I was never much of a student and I was absolutely abysmal at Cooking and Cleaning. Didn't care enough to make effort in Stealing and just failed. Nobody in my class passed Foolishness."

"I thought I could at least pass Drinking. Everyone else seemed to do fine, and just when I started having fun at last, it all turned miserable and now I've made a fool of myself."

"At least you earned points for Foolishness," Brody said.

"That might be the only class I'm good at. Drinking, Sensuality, Manipulation, I'm all horrible at," she said.

"Don't drink so fast next time," Brody advised.

"There won't be a next time," said Emile firmly, remembering how she looked in the mirror. "I'm not even certain I want my certificate."

"You do," Brody assured. "There's nothing here for you if you don't."

"You're still here."

"Only because Godfrey offered me a few nights here after he kicked me out. I was Fool enough to agree, so he made it a full time gig. I got lucky is what it was. He needed someone to manage the place."

"What about somewhere else? Surely this town isn't the only place in the world," said Emile.

"It's not," Brody said slowly.

"Then why don't you leave?" she asked.

"Can you think of a better place to go?" he smiled. "Besides, I'm a little older than you. It's not so easy to start over at my age."

"That's not true! How old are you?"

"Twenty-six," he said, meeting her eyes oddly.

Emile balked. "Brody, that's nothing! You have your whole life ahead of you! You could even go back to Lom and get your certificate. I'm sure you'd pass all the classes now," she said.

Under his beard he gave her a wry smile. "But who would watch over Godfrey?"

"Godfrey's an adult. He can watch over himself!"

"You're right," he said, throwing a glance at the passed

out owner. "But try keep it down, it'll be worse for you if you wake him."

"It's almost peaceful when it's this quiet," she said, looking around. The remaining patrons were all at least twenty years Brody's senior.

"Almost," Brody said, grabbing a set of keys off a hook behind the counter in a manner desensitized after years to the nature of a night at the bar.

"Do you need to throw up again?"

"No," Emile blushed.

"You will. Let's get you to your room, I won't make you walk back so late at night. Just let it be our little secret," he glanced at Godfrey again.

Brody led her up rough wooden stairs to the unlit second floor and into a narrow hallway, pushed open a door charily, somewhat small and as rough as the stairs, to a sparse guest bedroom with a bed, a stand and lamp beside it, a chest against the opposite wall. He lit the lamp before wishing her goodnight and closing the door behind him rather quickly.

Emile sat on the rough wool duvet but could not fall asleep. Her still sobering mind fell back to those swirling moments by the bathroom. She had lost her chance to find the wanderer. She had lost control and ended up humiliated.

Emile scanned the room for anything to write on, finding scrap papers and a couple rolling pencils inside the little drawer by her bed. She scrawled, pushing herself up closer to the waning candlelight:

Dear Wanderer,

You were so close to me tonight! I could feel it! It was you who led me here! If I hadn't followed you, I never would have stumbled into the Clown and the Bard, Godfrey never would have seen me and put me on the list, I never would have fallen into this strange world where everything I've learned is wrong!

By my very nature, I'm a foreigner here. I can't manipulate people or lie to my friends. I can't steal. When I first saw Lillian, my heart filled up with joy for the first time since we'd left Locronan, but she's one of them! She grew up here – I should have realized it. But all of these realizations about this place have been coming to me too late. I don't understand how it works, how the people here work. Everything the teachers say isn't what they really mean, but somehow Lillian and Dorian, Jesa and Max, understand what it is they're saying like it's

second nature. It's not my *second nature.
Everything one needs to earn the certificate is the
opposite of what's in me! Why, then, am I here?*

*I'm writing you right now from the very bar you
led me to. Lillian led us through the maze I got lost
in the night I saw you, which she knows like the
back of her hand, and I recognized the bar's door. I
think nobody believed me when I pointed it because
they all stood behind me like they were scared – but
what do they have to be afraid of? They're naturals
in this place. It's moments like these that I think
we're working together and we're friends, but the
next hour, they had me cornered as a way to get
points in Lying in Manipulation! Lillian, who keeps
saying she's my friend! I thought they wanted to
find the bar to drink, but they wanted points in
everything. Dorian, of all people, explained it to me.*

*I have nobody here to talk to. Even Brody, who I
thought was more like me because he failed his
certificate, ended up working in the bar. He was the
one who got us drunk! He's as much of Lom as any
of the teachers!*

*You are the only one here who is lost like me,
and I must find you. I found your door through the*

school. I saw your sign! The lantern and the star –
the same light you were carrying down the street
the night I chased you. I'll leave you this letter and
hope you write back. Slip your letter under the door
that leads up to the school. Tell me where I can
meet you. Tell me who you are! Tell me where I am
and why I've ended up in this strange place.

    Your friend,

    Emile

Satisfied, Emile folded the letter in half and placed it under her shirt. She could take no risks.

The heavy curtain across the window did its job; she slept through the night in one great sleep and when she awoke, she believed it was the middle of the night.

Godfrey had been removed somehow from his corner and Brody was nowhere to be seen, but the beer spills from last night were no more and most of the tipped over chairs had been righted.

Standing in the bar, she recalled the night's conversation and a different ache from the one in her head hit her, this time in the gut. Brody hadn't been intimating with her about life's trials and tribulations; he'd been watching over a fifteen-year-old girl who'd gotten drunk for the first time and imposed her idealism onto a man ten years older and thirty years wiser than she. The worms inside nullified the bright day beyond whose light fell through the windows, between the legs of upturned stools resting on silent tables, among last night's ghosts whose chatter replayed inside the cavern where her memories lived in a haze, becoming monsters they were not beyond reach of the light that fed and renewed the natural world, but not the world within her, where it was barred from entering while these newly minted demons fought their war.

The notion of the wanderer seemed ridiculous now in the face of daylight silence and a bubbling, ceaseless life out on the streets. Her moments with Brody were not at all as she had appraised them. Morning made that much clear.

She slipped carefully out to blend into the bright world, squinting from the sun almost nigh above her to locate the hill with its towering castle nestled behind full canopies of early summer. Emile trekked back in equal parts anger and anticipation, humiliated from her spectacular failure at Drinking, slipping in even more carefully than she'd left the bar and stealing straight to the library, where she made the journey to the wanderer's door again holding back several urges to vomit.

There it stood in the tunnel as before, affirming Emile like an embrace. No light shone from the other side. Emile gave a few clear knocks and slipped the letter underneath before turning around.

In the coming weeks, Emile often noticed Lillian, Dorian, Jesa, and Max huddled together at breakfast on Saturdays, red-eyed and sick but with triumphant expressions from their newfound Friday nights at the Clown and the Bard, where they snuck off after dinner to drink with Godfrey and the rest and became privy to the true goings-on in the castle. In the low lights, clad in the gaudiest getup and three drinks in, they listened with mimicked shrewd gazes as the teachers discussed the faults and dealings of so many characters in the castle and around town, including the students themselves, dropping hints about the direction of the classes that their eager ears chewed on. Try though they might not to make an entity of themselves and arouse curiosity over what tantalizing centerpiece bonded them so tightly, going so far as to arrive at the dining table separately and spend most of the morning talking amiably to others, including Emile, they inevitably found each other later in the morning. It didn't need a top student to notice the different quality about these intimations – the same seating arrangement they took up, the smaller head-neck angles, the secretive smiles over the sordid and unbelievable adventures from the night before.

Emile knew that all this meant their continued jaunts because she had been there once and some snippets of their murmured conversations made sense to her, but other students could easily brush off those curious moments, for they snuffed out all hint of their treasured underworld entirely during class.

"Did you guys sneak out on Friday?" Barton asked during Monday morning's Stealing class after their first trip to the bar, from which Emile still carried a bad taste in her mouth. "I looked all over the castle for you."

Dorian and Max shared looks of confusion and mild shock.

"I already told you I didn't find any liquor," Dorian said with a straight and dispassionate face that was disturbingly honest.

"I went to sleep ," said Max.

Barton looked to Emile sitting behind Dorian for confirmation of this unlikely story. Behind him, Dorian and Max looked at her as well, not intimidatingly, but with a patient wait for her reply.

"I went to sleep, too," she mumbled, not finding her tone

believable at all. "Godfrey was guarding the door."

She could see Barton's disappointment and reluctant acceptance beside the clear pleasure that came over the other two.

"Well I never told you – I found a ton of bottles hidden in someone's desk! but they were all empty," Barton said.

"What good will empty bottles do us in Drinking?" Max said.

"Don't be a bottle-half-empty man, empty bottles were full once," Dorian said to Max. "We'll find more."

"Tonight?" Barton asked.

"No way. They won't be partying on a Monday night," Dorian said truthfully. "Probably not until Friday. We'll look then."

"Whose desk was it?" asked Max.

"I'm not sure," Barton said.

"That information's useless to me," Emile saw Max's disappointment in being unable to arm himself with a potential bartering chip for next time he went to the bar.

Barton spent much of the rest of Stealing devising a search plan for Friday, costing him points in the class and double points for failing to score in a different class than the one they were in.

Emile, on the other hand, had earned points in Lying and Manipulation, much to Dorian's delight.

"Told you... a grain," he smirked next to her as they walked out and she held tightly onto all her belongings.

"Why didn't you tell him?" she asked quietly.

Dorian snorted. "Same reason you didn't. You don't want the secret out."

"I don't care."

"Keep fooling yourself. I won't be surprised to see you there next Friday."

"Good job keeping secrets yourself."

"Oh I'm not waiting until Friday to go back! Keep up, Emile!" he snapped his fingers and sped on ahead of her to their next class.

Their classes had progressed rapidly to more complex lessons, introducing such nuanced units as False Friendships and Opportunistic Put-Downs, both of which Emile struggled to keep up with. She always lagged several days behind; by the time she wrapped her head around the theory, the rest of the class had been practicing for a week, and on her; two days too late she registered Lillian and Jesa's recent upturn in friendliness for nothing but practice for False Friendship. She kicked herself for letting her trusting nature best her common sense yet again in spite of their earlier proven insincerity.

More and more each day, the students were molded in their teachers' images thanks to the constant pressure to stay nearest the top. They formed front-facing friendships, tripping each other for points at the first opportunity and resuming their friendship without mention of the betrayal, if it was even known. Extra points were awarded if it wasn't. It was impossible to know who sat at the top at any given moment. Victories were won in silence, in the dark, sometimes known to the victor and Godfrey alone.

These unknowable rankings being their constant concern, the class developed alliances and split into factions. Talk at mealtimes never started deeper than surface pleasantries until a few people threw each other heavy glances and bunched up to discuss something in briefly lowered voices. These intimacies were short lived and switched often, popping up as needed and fading to be forgotten, and the observable alliances spoke to little of truth. As she walked through the halls, the classrooms, mealtimes, Emile could not distinguish between who liked each other and who hated each other; she only knew that nobody knew where they stood with each other, even among those at the top. Lillian alone appeared to work expertly in this pool of colliding molecules, deftly forming and breaking her bonds like a dancer. She pulled Jesa aside to discuss Dorian's next move one morning, and walked arm in arm with Dorian confiding her suspicions of Jesa that same afternoon.

Emile maintained a defensive posture, learning the techniques at a minimum only to satisfy her daily interactions. She didn't steal, but she knew how not to be stolen from; she did not seduce, but she knew how not to repel; she did not manipulate others, but she recognized when she was being manipulated and redirected it. She did her best to balance gleaning points with giving up as little of herself as she could to these despicable arts, leveling out on the whole to a C-average student. She wrote of her findings and revelations to the wanderer every week, even though she never received a response:

> *Dear Wanderer,*
>
> *The students are divided into the leaders and the followers. The leaders are Dorian, Lillian, Max, Jesa. They are the top of the class, the best manipulators, the most sensually persuasive.*

Stealing for them is breathing. But above all, they go to the Clown and the Bard.

The rest of the class are followers. They play according to the rules and know nothing of what truly goes on. They believe the story they are told and continue to learn what cannot be learned by the book, by the book! They don't see that there is a deeper layer beneath the castle. They go to their classes and their rooms. The Clown and the Bard is just a rumor to them. But do they ever wonder where Godfrey and Jacqueline go after class? Do they ever question why the castle becomes so quiet after hours and they never see anyone? No. They take everything at face value.

It's frightening to see that at first that was my tendency, too. Had I never accidentally fallen into that bar, I would be just like them! Had I never followed you, I would still be living a lie. I might still believe Lillian to be my friend.

The leaders think they know the teachers because they drink with them and listen to their stories, but they are just as deluded as the rest in this regard! Godfrey is as much of a mystery to them as to anyone else, and Jacqueline has a power over

Lillian that renders her helpless! Lillian, the girl
who is never manipulated, who is perfectly
acceptable in every social maneuver, wants nothing
more than Jacqueline's approval!

I am not one of the leaders, but neither am I one
of the followers. I don't know who I am.

Emile's distance from the game earned her many glances from the core group. Slowly she became aware that she was a mystery to them; why didn't she frequent the Clown and the Bard? Any other student would have killed for the knowledge. Within the castle, the bar tantalized the class like a legend, one the teachers casually sneered at. But a few lived the legend in truth, and their surreptitiously exchanged darts of meaning with the teachers were real. They treated the rest of the class like the unenlightened, but they could not act that way toward Emile, for she, too knew about the Clown and the Bard.

After some time it occurred to Emile that in fact they were, as she thought she'd imagined, keeping their distance, for she had made plainly clear to Dorian that she placed no value in the certificate or in learning the secrets of Lom. It was her one bit of leverage: she could at a moment's notice reveal the Clown and the Bard's existence and open the floodgates, an ability she hinted at from time to time, not intentionally, but simply by being herself in a place such as this. Thus she and the insiders formed an unspoken pact. She helped them maintain their insider status, and in turn she gained a degree of immunity in their classes.

This tentative equilibrium frustrated Dorian. Emile had found a major weakness in him and them, and now she, one, balanced the weight of them, four. His dissatisfaction with her status naturally led him to more careful observations of her tactics, and it wasn't long before he caught the first hints of her deeper concerns.

Gunter was charged with giving the students an allowance, a task he carried out every morning during *Stealing*. He walked around the room and handed each of them one gold coin, which most instinctively stowed to hoard for their sunny afternoons about town. It became an obsession; people spent their lives in and out of class guarding their fluctuating piles at the cost of their other classes, which they forgot about in the ensuing paranoia that gripped most.

Dorian and Max, as usual, hardly fretted. They were loose with their gold because, in their eyes, they had a whole classroom of gold if they wanted it. Emile, too, took a different approach, letting a controlled trickle of coins get stolen so that her pile never grew too large for her to maintain or for the others to be tempted by, all the while trying to game it so that her coins spread among the less fortunate and kept the wealthy slightly less so. While flaunting this savior flair, she was effectively able to keep the true size of her pile hidden, but one behavior she could not hide was that she herself never stole. Sensing this, Emile stole a coin one day from Barton, who was always down on his. And the next day, she let Barton steal one from her. Sensing also that their tenuous alliance had not gone unseen, she did not repeat this behavior until next week when she let Barton steal from her two days in a row, and the following week, she stole her two coins rather easily back with no sign of indignation on his part.

After that came a period of time particularly hard for the poor, as always happened was when the class applied Stealing's newest lesson. By the middle of that week many were down to their last coin, Emile among them, and instinctively hunkered down to weather their precarious position until tomorrow, keeping close guard over their last lifeline and taking a hit on other fronts just to survive.

"Go for the low hanging fruit. Don't be afraid," Dorian mumbled by her ear that morning while she sat tensely hunchbacked in her chair, waiting for *Stealing* to end. He shot a glance at Barton, seated similarly but looking both eager and hopeless.

"I'm not afraid," Emile said. But this was untrue; like the rest, Emile feared leaving her desk and stepping into the open field lest her last possession be swiftly taken. She feared execution.

"Some people don't have to betray their friends to win at a game," she took the high ground.

Dorian laughed. "Don't be naïve. He'd betray you in a heartbeat if a better arrangement came along."

"So I should betray him before he betrays me?"

"Emile gets the day's lesson the day it's given!" he sounded more like Godfrey with each passing day.

"That attitude is exactly what *creates* the behavior you're trying to counter!" she said.

Dorian's grin did not falter. He called Barton over, something that hadn't happened in *Stealing* in weeks. In surprise, the weak-bodied boy held his coin close and hobbled over to sit by Dorian and Max.

"Fancy plans this weekend?" Dorian asked him genially.

"Why?" Barton was visibly apprehensive with two pairs of hungry eyes upon him.

"Thought you might want to go for a drink," Dorian said in a hushed voice.

Barton's eyes widened and he leaned in, gripping his coin more tightly. "*Did you... did you find the bar*? Or do you want to...?"

Dorian rubbed two gold coins in his fingers. "Why do you think we're getting these? Bars won't be open Saturday lunch, but liquor stores will."

"Who's going to sell you liquor?" Barton laughed.

"Who wouldn't sell liquor to someone willing to pay three times the price?" Dorian countered.

"What were *you* gonna use your gold for?" Max asked defensively to Barton's look.

"It's not pretty but we have to do what we have to do," said Dorian with steel.

"I won't tell anyone you paid three times the amount for your alcohol," Barton grinned.

"If you do we'll deny it," Max said.

Emile watched their exchange out of the corner of her eye; Barton slowly relaxed after neither Dorian nor Max made any indication to steal from him, diplomatically avoiding the invitations to strike down vulnerability as if they weren't dancing in their laps. In fact they had no intention at all to steal from Barton, and Barton sensed this. What he did not sense was the bigger picture, and Emile sensed it only too late.

"So, do you want in?" Dorian asked with the air of finally getting to the point.

"Well, *yeah*."

"Great. Saturday – "

"What do I have to do?" Barton asked.

"Split the cost," said Max. "Duh. We're not funding your drinking habit."

Barton stayed hushed for a moment. "Sorry. I don't think I can help."

"We only need five more," Dorian said.

"*Only five?*" A look of shame overcame Barton's face. "I don't think I've ever *had* five coins. I don't get how you guys do it."

"You want to know our secret?" Dorian said, and Emile tensed up, waiting for them to pounce on their target.

But the tension dissipated. "We set a combined goal of six and we throw it into the pot and split down the middle. That's how we always have so many."

"So you each try and get three? That's not a secret strategy."

Dorian shook his head. "We don't each try and get three. We try to get *six*, *together*. Some days I get more, some days Max gets more. But we figure, overall, it evens out. And we always get six."

"At least," added Max. "Well we *did*. But as we've improved, we've raised the stakes."

"To what?" Barton asked slowly.

"Double."

"*Twelve*?" they had to hush Barton hastily.

"That's how we're gonna win Drinking before anyone else," Dorian muttered.

"How many do you have?" Barton asked, finally catching on.

"Ten. So if you have *two coins*, we'll let you in on it."

"You think I'm an idiot? You'll just take my coins," Barton said.

"Have you been paying attention to this conversation – " Max started before Dorian cut him off.

"We could. You're right. *But* – if we do, are you likely to help us in the future?"

"Obviously not," said Barton.

"Right. But if you do, and we split twelve coins, we each get four. And we *continue* to get four. Or five, if we get even better! It's your call," Dorian said neutrally.

"I want to do it," Barton said quietly. "I can give one today, but tomorrow I'll get more," he held up his last.

"One? Look... we have each other's backs and all, but you've got to pull your weight!" Dorian said.

Disappointment overcame the poor boy. "Sorry," he walked back to his desk. But when Emile looked back to where she secured her usual small pile of coins, not one was there.

She stared at Barton, dumbfounded, as he dropped two coins into Dorian's hand, but he merely shrugged.

"It's Stealing, Emile. Anyway, lighten up, it's just a class," Barton said.

"Last coin? Cold as ice, Barton!" Dorian clapped him on the back, impressed.

"Class is about over. Let's show Gunter while we've got them," said Barton.

"We'll take care of it," said Max. "See if you can get more, make up your contribution."

"But – "

"Don't worry about it," Max assured.

"*Double* points for Max and Dorian today!" Gunter exclaimed at the impressive pile of twelve gold coins the two showed him. "One minute left! If your pile is empty, you've lost your allowance."

Neither of them acknowledged Barton, who now looked as dumbfounded as Emile had a moment ago, but to Emile Dorian threw a pointed grin.

"I should have known this would happen," Barton said sheepishly, turning to her. She felt an initial pang of pity, but a new storm welled up in revolt and crashed over the first with unprecedented violence. Without hesitation she grabbed the very last coins of three nearby students sitting in dejection. It was a weak, cheap meal, dinner for bottom feeders, a desperate, ugly maneuver, and she took it without pity.

Dorian watched her with supreme satisfaction. Nobody stole final coins; it meant fewer people to steal from in the future.

"Not a bad start!" Dorian couldn't suppress his smile, but it shrunk quickly to mere amusement as Emile threw her coins onto his desk and marched out of *Stealing*.

Furious with herself and with Lom once more, Emile marched straight to the library after *Stealing* to intimate to her dearest companion, skipping the rest of their classes.

Dear Wanderer,

I feel sick to my stomach: for the first time I stole, and not just stole; I took the last coins of the poorest students and took three people out of the game. I justified it because I was furious, because Dorian had manipulated Barton, who I thought was my friend, to steal from me. But that was my own fault: how many times must I learn that nobody is a friend? I understand more and more each day what you need to do to survive here, but it kills me! This school goes against everything I've ever been taught! My whole life I've been taught not to steal, and now to pass I must do the opposite. I remind myself again and again that you must be cold and hardened to survive here and slowly, slowly but surely, I become that.

The sickening part was that I played right into Dorian's trap. He wanted to prove that I'm no better than the rest and today he did. I don't want to admit it, but I'm a little proud of what I did today because

I finally proved that I could do it! And, you know, there's no secret. The secret is to have no shame! That's it! If Godfrey evaluated me tomorrow I would still be out on the streets, but somewhere there is a border between the fear of failure and the desire for success, and today I crossed it.

Before this, I haven't had to steal, or manipulate, or try and seduce anyone (as if I could!). I've been able to get by just avoiding all of it being done on me... but the truth is, I like being able to dodge their tricks! Does it really make me better if I still like the game? I like guessing when Dorian is going to try and manipulate me. I laugh to myself whenever Lillian gives me a hug and while hugging her back, I try to figure out what she really wants.

Is it inevitable that to get that certificate I will kill off my softer nature? For a piece of paper stating Godfrey's approval of what I've become? It's disgusting what atrocities the students – soon to be adults! – will commit against each other for a man's approval! I worry that in becoming acceptable to the Skola Lom I am losing myself.

She emerged from the little doorway and rounded the

corner when the presence of Dorian made her gasp. He looked utterly unsurprised to see her.

"Shouldn't you be in class? Or out buying liquor?" she fired, trying to smooth out the signs of disturbance on her face.

"I was in the mood to read. Any good books in that corner?" Dorian peered curiously around the shelf to the back corner, having spotted Emile there twice now. Her heart leaped right back up.

"Go see for yourself," she moved out of the way and ushered him down.

"Another day."

An unexpected pause fell between them and Emile moved past him down the shelves.

"You going to spend all day in the library?"

"What's it to you?" asked Emile, suddenly self-conscious that he was more aware of her whereabouts than she'd realized.

"I'm just trying to help you."

"I've had enough of your help for one day," she walked by.

"I wanted to apologize for Stealing," he said.

"Right."

"It's true!"

"Apology accepted," she said emptily, pulling off a curious looking book.

"I haven't apologized yet. I can't give you back your coins, 'cause that's bad for me, but I can offer to convert them into drinks. I know for a fact you're failing Drinking," he said."And after Stealing today..."

"I don't care – "

"Yeah, you don't care about the certificate. We all know. But think about if Godfrey kicks you out of the school? He said you're out the same night. How are you going to pay for a ticket back with no coins?" Dorian posed for her.

"I'd think Godfrey would get us – " but she stopped herself, realizing her assumption was ridiculous.

Godfrey had never mentioned providing any ticket out of Lom, and if Emile knew Godfrey, he would likely turn it into another test.

"So you apologize with so many drinks that you humiliate me in front of the teachers and leave me in the bathroom again to get points for Manipulation?"

"I'll make sure you don't drink too much this time. I

promise."

But Emile had been fooled too many times and he knew this.

"If I do anything like that, you can tell Barton about the bar. You have one over me," he said. Emile nodded slowly to herself as his motivation at last became clear. Yet he was close to getting one over her. He had glimpsed her attachment to this part of the library, and she did not want to feed his nascent inklings further with any inexplicable behavior.

"No one will be there when it's not even dark. What do you have to lose? You might even have fun, who knows."

"Alright," she agreed.

"Good!" Dorian grabbed her hand and pulled her out of the library.

"How did you know I'd be in the there?" Emile asked when they were safely beyond the castle's confines and walking through the quiet evening streets upon which the sun had long set.

"I have common sense, Emile. I don't get it. You're smart, you know that life in the castle is bullshit for people like Barton. Why do you stay there?"

"The library's the farthest place from that world," she

answered.

"You're the only one who knows about the Clown and the Bard and doesn't go!" Dorian exclaimed as if he'd been waiting a month to say this.

"It's not exactly my place."

"Any bar isn't exactly your place," he chuckled.

It struck Emile as they walked into town together that in the real world she and Dorian would pass each other by without a word. But here they were, opposites incarnate, brought side by side by circumstance. Dorian was an alien mind, a glimpse into another world that she would never otherwise see. Would they revert to being strangers who knew nothing of each other outside the confines of the school?

The bar was quiet as he had promised. None of their teachers were yet there. Besides the two of them, a few older men Emile didn't recognize took up seats at the bar, each evoking varying stages of Godfrey in appearance but with none of his charisma or vivaciousness. Brody leaned against the counter talking to two of them. In the middle, the collection of circular tables displayed their pockmarked, chipped, and scuffed surfaces today. Only two had occupants, each a quietly talking pair.

Dorian waved to one of the elderly men at the end of the bar as to an old friend as he exchanged two coins for two beers.

"Don't tell me the library's a better escape than this," he smiled, leaning back and taking an easy sip of his beer as he surveyed the scene.

"This isn't an escape, it's a deeper level of the game! It's a town full of people who gossip and deceive each other and have not one true friend, and we're being groomed to be like them," Emile said. She straightened up and took a sip of her own beer, tasting its bitterness for the first time.

"That's why it's the best place to get practice for class. Spend a few nights here and you'll be the top manipulator."

"But I don't *want* to be the top manipulator. Why would anyone want that? To constantly be on edge, making sure your supposed friends aren't pulling the rug out from under your feet?"

"It's not that we want to; it's the way of the world," Dorian said matter of factly. "Godfrey's preparing us for what's after school. Don't you see? Kids who go to normal schools will come out and they'll get manipulated and stolen from their first day, but not us."

Emile took another sip. "It's not the way of my world."

For a moment Dorian looked at her with tenderness, but wiped it off quickly.

"I know what your problem is," he said.

"I don't need another drink."

"You're afraid you *can't* pass the classes. You were so smart in Locronan but out here you don't know how to do it!"

"I hate what we have to do," she defended, but she blushed, struck by his accurate aim.

"Would you hate it as much if it came easy to you?"

Emile thought about it. She knew that much of the fuel for her impassioned letters to the wanderer was a direct result of the anger and embarrassment she felt from her shortsighted mishaps in the classrooms. And she wanted to believe that as a top student she would still keep her position against Lom, but it occurred to her that if she *were* a top student, she would value everything differently.

"You're not as bad at it as you think you are," Dorian said to her silence. "You just always stay on the outside. And that's your weakness: not the lessons themselves, that you're alone. You don't want to be allied with anyone."

Emile snorted. "No one is allied with anyone. Even you! You didn't invite Lillian and Jesa and even Max here!"

"I'm a free agent, not joined at the hip like Jesa and Lillian. I'm like you... I mean, you're like me."

"I am not. You *relish* being on the inside!"

"And you relish being on the outside! Admit it, Emile, you like watching the game from afar and knowing what's about to happen." Dorian shook his head. "Sometimes we think you might secretly be the best in the class," he said.

"What?" she raised her eyebrows.

"But then we interact and I get my head on straight."

They both laughed.

"Even if I knew how to be the best, I'd never do what it takes," said Emile.

"It's not as hard as you're making it seem," Dorian said. "You just have to keep a few keys in mind. They're like shortcuts!"

"Oh?"

He pulled his stool toward hers and faced her, talking in the smaller space between them with his hands.

"Take Stealing. Why do you think the same people keep getting coins and the same people keep losing them?"

"Because some people are good at Stealing," said Emile.

Dorian shook his head.

"It has nothing to do with someone's skill or talent. It's their mindset. Everyone getting stolen from is on the defensive. They're *protecting* their coins."

"What choice do they have when people like you would steal them at the first chance?"

"It's not the stealers but the fear of losing what you have that keeps you where you are! The truth is, you're actually safer stepping into the open field and risking losing what you have than you are hiding. But you can never understand that until you make the leap."

"That means jumping right into the jaws of predators."

"That's why it's a secret! It's counterintuitive. The way out is right *to* the jaws of death," he smiled.

"Easy to say for someone born on the other side," said Emile. "You didn't have to jump across...."

Dorian gave a one sided grin. "You seem to know a lot about where I was born."

"You're from Paris."

"Only for a year, with my aunt and uncle while my parents traveled. I grew up in Trient. That's where I was born."

"What's that, some village population three hundred?"

Emile said mockingly.

"One fifty," he corrected.

"You're lying."

"I don't always have to lie to win in Lying and Manipulation. Another key," he said pointedly. "Ask me anything about it."

"Describe it."

"Beautiful. Hidden away in the mountains, big blue sky, friendly people, simple food. You could see Mont Blanc."

"What did you do there?"

"Oh, lots of things. There wasn't much to do in the way of entertainment besides go to the bar, but there was a lot of land. I remember sledding most of all. I doubt you'd find better sledding, or rock climbing. Sometimes people got together and played music. And of course there were sports."

"That sounds like a good life," Emile said. She was forcibly reminded by his stories of her own childhood.

"It was. I loved growing up there."

"Don't you want to go back?" she looked around the old bar, unable to see what Dorian saw in it.

He shrugged. "I'm a long way from that life. After years of traveling and seeing new things you forget about the little village."

Emile's heart dropped. For the first time, she saw herself reflected in Dorian. For all her longing and yearning to return to a simpler time would she, too, simply forget the fast fading riches of her idyllic childhood and never return?

"But it's home," she said.

"It is, but there's more out there than home."

"Like what? Having the inside scoop on an underworld full of sordid secrets?"

"That stuff is in Locronan, too," Dorian said wryly. "You just didn't see it."

Emile shook her head emphatically, impassioned now by the drink. "It's *not* the same. People in Locronan had true friends. They held on to what was best in life. What's the appeal of the teachings of Lom over what you could have in Locronan? I can't understand! I may be a naïve village girl, but I know one thing, and it's that places like Locronan are places people spend their entire lives searching for. In a place like this, how is friendship possible?... How is love possible?"

A caravan burst through the front door. Godfrey led the way in full force and color, arm in arm with a laughing Jacqueline wrapped in a falling sparkling shawl. Gunter followed, roaring deeply with Betsy twirling in gauze behind him. Lillian, Jesa, and Max came after the parade like miniatures. Ghost-like Gaunt brought up the rear, closing the door before falling silently off the train and fading into the wall as usual as the bar quickly came to life.

"Emile! What a surprise!" Lillian smiled briskly and hugged her as a round of shots appeared for the five students.

"Finally partying with us again!" Max grinned at Dorian, who had jumped off his stool the moment the party arrived. Emile remained sitting, her comprehension lagging behind events.

"Well look who joined us!" Godfrey roared, throwing his arms around Dorian and Emile as he rounded to the bar and joined them in a toast. Emile took only a sip from her glass and hung on to it.

"Building up a good tolerance?" Godfrey asked her.

"This one's a regular, stick with him you'll be an expert drinker in no time," said Gunter, clapping Dorian on the back. Dorian stumbled forward, already tipsy, but flushed with pleasure.

Brody appeared with another round for the two men and the two boys. Dorian, worse off than the rest, held his own with them.

Emile couldn't stand the absurdity. "Stop, you're making him sick! He's only sixteen!" she cried.

"And he's only sixteen!" Godfrey roared, hoisting his shot in one hand and his tankard in the other. Emile watched in pain as Dorian took the shot and finished the rest of Godfrey's beer. Brody placed another one in front of him immediately.

"*You've* got some work to do," Godfrey wagged a finger in Emile's face.

Jacqueline had taken up her usual table and brought out her bag of accessories. She and Betsy pulled out sequined masks and donned them over their eyes; through the small slits, they needed not tear their gazes away from the sights too often to stay discreet. Lillian and Jesa gathered beside them and immediately followed suit, Lillian pulling out a crown with glee and ramming it onto her head while Jesa reached for a veil and a large heart shaped pendant on a chain. In fitting costumes, they took up stools at the women's table to watch the unfolding drunkenness on display by the bar.

"Looks like Godfrey's settled on his protégé," Betsy said with some amusement.

"I haven't seen him so pleased since he was mentoring Brody," Jacqueline observed coolly.

"Brody used to be Godfrey's protégé?" Lillian devoured.

"Godfrey always needs a protégé," Jacqueline and Betsy said simultaneously.

Both women sipped on their drinks and watched Godfrey, dancing now *on* the bar. Neither one flinched when he nearly fell over, but Dorian's hand for a moment did, prompting Gunter and Brody's laughter and assurance that Godfrey always stumbled and never fell. A moment later, Godfrey toppled, caught by the floor with the thunderous crashing of wood and flesh upon stone peppered with shrieks and howls that gave way to more laughter, drawing chuckles even from Betsy. Locals now joined their entourage, filling up the space between the bar and the table with chatter and drink.

"Ladies! What's this sideline collusion?" Godfrey cried from behind them, throwing one arm over Betsy and one over Jacqueline. "There's no secrets in a bar!"

"You're under dressed," Betsy said.

"Indeed I am, my fair friend!" Godfrey cried,

immediately pulling a matted lion's mane out of Jacqueline's bag.

Lillian and Jesa dove back into the treasure trove, pulling out costume after costume and roaming around the crowd, adorning the participants into the court they were building. Emile watched every patron become a member of the kingdom. Dorian had disappeared out of sight. A small sense of dread rose in her as she stood alone by the bar amid strange lords and ladies, wily merchants and ragged travelers. Who was missing? Who did they need? At once it made sense. She knew why she was brought here, knew what she'd walked into in her trusting blindness.

A gentle tug at her side came from Jesa, who hugged her and draped a woolen cape over her shoulders before Lillian, approaching grandly, made to slip the clown collar over her head.

"No!" Emile yelled, pushing her out of the way and knocking her crown off. "I'm not here to be your clown!"

Everyone in the vicinity stood back and some grew quiet. They looked at each other in confusion, as if Emile had yelled in a foreign language.

"What's wrong?" Jesa asked.

"I'm not wearing that," said Emile.

"Well here, pick something else," Lillian handed her the bag.

"No. I've had enough for one night," she took off the cape and turned to go.

"Leaving just as an epic night is starting? Do you know how many points you'll lose?" said Dorian as everybody watched her disbelievingly.

"That's *unheard* of," said Lillian with great disappointment.

"Party pooper," said Max. "Even Barton knows you don't do that."

"You'll have just as much fun without me," Emile assured.

"No we won't," Dorian said, deflated. "Whatever, have fun at the library."

She caught Godfrey's expression of supreme disappointment beneath his jester's cap, watching her soberly from the corner of the bar as she walked out. Emile was not foolish enough to be used a second time.

She returned to the castle, penning and delivering a second letter to her companion safe in the knowledge that no one would look for her. Once more no response letter waited on her side and the door remained stubbornly shut, a dim light behind its cracks now tantalizing her as it always did when she visited in the evenings.

Dear Wanderer,

I am at a crossroads. I don't know how to think of what is happening anymore. Am I being made a fool of, or am I the one being a fool? Do I see a hidden truth or have I gone mad with my perceptions? The longer I stay here, the harder it is to tell.

After today's incident in Stealing, Dorian found me in the library and convinced me to go to the bar. He skipped class to look for me and he knew exactly where I would be! Not that skipping class would affect him. Maybe it was even better for his scores in some way I don't understand in the way I don't understand anything *at Lom.*

I cannot reconcile my interactions here. I know perfectly well how the people are, but in spite of all the evidence, sometimes I feel we truly connect. There are moments when I feel that Lillian is sincere with me. And sometimes I catch Dorian hesitating and see his doubts. I don't know if it's guilt or remorse or something else, but sometimes a little thought strikes me that he, too, wishes for a different way than what we're taught. For the tiniest moments he seems touched by something I do or say, but it's as if he tramples upon it immediately. Tonight in our moments alone he struck a chord with me, but the second everybody else showed up, it turned out he had manipulated me! He had brought me as their fool! Was this the truth all along, even during our conversation?

Am I the naïve one making up fantasies? It's not that I'm duped – I know exactly what's going on! – it's that I still have hope that somewhere, in those parts of the students I bond with, lives something that has not been drowned out by louder voices. It seems hopeless. Dorian is Godfrey's protege like Lillian is Jacqueline's. They want nothing more than to be like them. They want it more than any connection, if that is something they want. It is I who can't remember to consider this fact before everything else.

Months had passed since their initiation into Lom, but nothing shocked them as much as when Godfrey afforded them a break. He surprised them the next morning at breakfast, canceling classes for the rest of the week and ordering them to return to their homes through the weekend.

"Stand outside and clear your heads," his booming voice rang.

Emile quickly packed her bags and followed the rest out of the castle in a still surprised line as Godfrey saw them off at the door, handing each one a train ticket as they passed.

"Emile," he said her name as he placed a ticket into her hand. Then he gave her a lingering look and added, "Take care to return."

It was one of the few times Emile saw the headmaster up close. His face was pale and tired, out of sync with his commanding voice.

Emile slipped into a lull out the window as soon as she boarded the train. With each mile of country that rolled by, the world of Lom crumbled more thoroughly behind her, leaving an unfettered clearing in its place. Dorian and Lillian, the fumbling nights at the bar, Godfrey's unbridled reign: all of it belonged to a dream world. Simple sunlight fell onto her face and for the first time since entering Lom she smiled freely.

Her mother nearly dropped the plate she was holding when Emile walked through the door early that evening.

"Emile!" she cried.

"The headmaster sent us home for the weekend."

Her mother pulled her into the tightest embrace she could remember. A season's build up of strain and anxiety fell from her shoulders as she stayed pressed to her mother's chest and her caring, elegant arms stroked her tenderly.

"I've been so worried. You haven't answered any of my letters! Are they keeping you that busy?"

"I haven't gotten any letters. We're not allowed to send or receive them. The headmaster wants us to break contact with anything outside school to focus on our studies."

Her mother's eyes widened. "I don't remember him being so stern."

"About some things," said Emile. "It's like no other school."

"I want to hear all about it. Why don't you get settled upstairs and join us for dinner. You'll love what we did with your room."

Emile had no energy for even the light switch. As soon as she dropped her bags on her bedroom floor she collapsed onto her bed in her clothes and slept through the night.

When she awoke, the same simple sunlight streamed onto her walls and over her soft blue quilt. Her mind was quiet. It was as if the past two months had never happened.

She joined her mother in the sunny kitchen, a little nook filled with bright yellow accents. Someone else was already sitting at the table: Emile's older cousin, holding a soft infant boy wrapped in a blanket.

"Adelaide and the baby arrived this morning! Isn't that a lovely surprise?" her mother beamed.

The young freckled face Emile hadn't seen in years smiled up at her like the bright young girl she remembered, now radiant in her newfound glow. Emile stood above the tiny, rosy-cheeked boy, who looked straight at her with unfettered deep blue eyes.

"Eat, dear, I'll take him," said Emile's mother as she scooped the infant from Adelaide, rubbing the innocent face that returned a smile in response. With the morning light falling over her soft brown waves and kind gaze, Emile's mother appeared an embodiment of infinite gentleness.

They spent the warm, cloudless day wandering the parks, reminiscing over memories from long before the baby's time. Emile took her turn pushing the stroller, consumed with watching her nephew's round eyes take in the world with unquestioning perception.

They returned early in the evening to prepare and prepare for dinner. Emile's mother readied in mere minutes, changing quickly into a simple cotton dress and halfway pinning her hair up before the boy's cries demanded her attention and she let go of the bun, letting the strands fall out messily.

The image of Jacqueline burst forth in her wild beauty as if violently unearthed, draped in sensuous fabrics over her shamelessly flaunted breast and her long, lithe arms. Emile saw her more clearly than she did at school when she stood beside her ineffectually clad mother: her dark locks shining like polished metal, her high, proud jutting cheekbones, her flashing dark eyes beneath clever eyebrows were harshly defined against her mother's fuzzy softness, which bore none of this arresting quality. At once Emile's shortcomings in Sensuality became crystal clear to her. Never once had she seen Jacqueline hummingly set a dinner table with a smile on her face. She could not imagine anything besides Jacqueline seating herself at a plate set *for* her in her queenly spot.

Tearing herself away from the vision, Emile marched to her bedroom and flung open her closet, staring at herself in the mirror. A knock came on her door some minutes later.

"Where'd you run off to – well you look fancy! Is that a corset?" asked Adelaide, admiring Emile as she put her hair up into a loose bun that showed off her long neck with a couple waving strands hanging down the sides of her face.

"It's just something I got in town one weekend," said Emile innocuously, smoothing the dress' lace sleeves down over her bared shoulders, but smiling to herself at her cousin's stupefied expression as she watched her. Like her mother, Adelaide wore a plain dress, and she'd put her hair into two country plaits that fell over her shoulders and already had strands poking out.

"Do you want me to watch the baby while you get ready?" Emile offered helpfully.

"Oh – I am ready," Adelaide laughed. "If I'd known we were dressing up I would have brought something fancier... not that I have anything *that* fancy."

"Do you want to borrow something? I have another corset," Emile offered.

"Oh, you're a little smaller than I am," Adelaide said.

"We can loosen it! I'm sure Marshall wouldn't mind if you wore it," Emile said slyly. Adelaide blushed.

"Your mother wanted you to come down for dinner," she mumbled.

"I'll be down in a minute," said Emile sweetly, making final adjustments to her hair. "Do you want me to fix your braids?" she offered.

"That's alright," Adelaide grabbed one and pulled back from Emile.

Emile came down alone as her father and Marshall's voices joined the ambient noise. Everyone was already seated and a plate waited for her at the table.

"Emile! What a lovely young woman you've become!" said Marshall, getting up from his chair and kissing her hand when she walked through. "When I saw you at our wedding you were just a girl. You're transformed!"

"Emile was just a girl last time *I* saw her," said her father, standing up and giving her a hug. "She's been away at school for the past two months."

Emile took a seat between Marshall and her mother.

"What have you been learning in school?" Marshall asked her.

"Fashion, it looks like," said her mother, noting her dress.

"Yes, we have," Emile said in earnest. "Not all learning comes from a book."

"My, you *have* learned," said her father.

Marshall chuckled. "Are you reading *any* books?"

"*Emmanuelle.*"

"What's that about?" Adelaide asked across the table as Marshall looked at Emile with surprise.

"You haven't heard of it?" Emile asked her.

"It wouldn't be your kind of book, dear," Marshall said to his wife.

"What's that supposed to mean?" Adelaide asked.

"It's a little risqué."

"It's an erotic novel," Emile clarified, speaking in a tone of maturity to handle such topics.

"You're reading that for class?" Marshall asked with amusement.

"We're studying it as a work of art in our twentieth century French literature class," said Emile smoothly, spinning an elaborate tale about the many controversial books they'd read and how they were taught to examine everything as art. She paraphrased a couple of quotes to prove she had read it, though she had not; they had studied about it in Sensuality during their Illusion of Culture unit, where they examined the covers, flipped through a few pages, and talked about who had read the book and what they had thought of it.

"Looking at it critically has really made me think more about how you can live your life," Emile said.

"In what way?" Emile's mother asked hesitantly.

"Well... do I *really* want to do what everyone does?"

"And what does everyone do?"

"You know... get married, have children, settle down into a family life."

"Those are wonderful things!" said her mother.

"But what if I don't ever want them? What if I never meet someone I want to marry or have kids with?"

"You will. You have plenty of time," her mother gave a little laugh, relieved at having understood Emile's budding adolescent anxieties.

"It's not time that's the problem. It's that, now I see most people do it because it's 'the thing to do', not out of love or because they really thought about what they wanted to do with their lives."

"There's some truth to that," said Marshall.

"Is there?" Adelaide asked him with a small degree of affront.

"Well, let's be honest, dear."

"It doesn't seem *bad*, it just seems limiting," continued Emile. "We have so many parts to ourselves, and different people bring out different parts! But when we fall into routines or remain with the same person, we might never know them!"

"Emile, you're too young to truly understand about any of that," said her mother. Her voice was far less sweet than before.

"I'm *not* too young anymore! I'm not saying marriage and children are *undesirable,* I'm saying there's so much to life that I wouldn't want to *do* that until I've, oh I don't know, had a great adventure, or really lived a life worth writing about. Once you become a mother, you can't be young anymore! Everything about youth starts to fade away."

"Motherhood is the most beautiful expression of womanhood there is," said her mother. "Look at Adelaide.... Look at me."

"What about women who never become mothers? Are they less women?" argued Emile. Nobody responded.

"The most beautiful woman I've seen was never a mother. But she's unbridled and free. She has a powerful and commanding manner. And she's not afraid of her own beauty. She knows how to use it."

"Use it?" asked her father.

"Where did you see this woman?" asked her mother.

"She's one of our teachers, Jacqueline."

Her mother made no reaction, and Emile went on at length about all of her teachers, regaling the table with carefully selected sights from the world she had been exposed to, but never mentioning the bar. She practiced her mastery over a crowd as Jacqueline had taught them, throwing her shoulders back and dropping her voice. She played with her sleeves, drawing attention to her bare shoulders, and when her mother brought out dessert, she ate it delicately with a sensuous savor. She saw Marshall throw her side glances, but made sure she didn't once glance back in his direction, staring forward for now as she had seen Jacqueline do. She felt herself scoring points on practically every subject: *Lying and Manipulation*, *Sensuality, False Friendship*, *Deceptive Image*; she hit nearly the entire syllabus.

After dessert, Adelaide put her son to bed while the rest of the family congregated around the fireplace for tea. Emile sat apart and examined them critically, remembering what Dorian had said about everything they found in Lom existing in Locronan, too. She stayed on alert throughout their friendly conversation, a diver looking for double meanings in restrained expressions, for signs of deception lingering like poison between her mother and father, for seemingly minor miscommunication forging an unstoppably widening rift between the new parents.

She dropped Jacqueline into the living room and tried to see them through her eyes. *What was it that made Marshall want to marry her cousin? She couldn't feed his intellectuality. He's stepping on himself every day to be beside her! Is she starting to realize, now that the newlywed shimmer has faded, that she can't give him everything he craves? That in constantly admiring her cuteness he is saying that he holds her more as a pet? No, Marshall doesn't this about himself yet. But he will. As their baby grows older, he sees himself and the world around him... and all the opportunities in it that he passed on. That is how they will stagnate,* Jacqueline's eyes told her.

And her parents – are they really so simple as they appear? Are they true to what they seem on the surface, or are their own conflicts simply deeper ingrained? Being born into them, could she even see them?

Emile looked hard at her mother sitting wrapped by her father's arm on the love seat, trying to answer the questions. They sat calmly, her mother listening serenely while her father discussed farming methods with Marshall.

Godfrey would have started a riot by now! she thought. *He wouldn't sit still. He'd be drinking and trying to get everyone in the bar to drink with him!* With sinking disappointment, Emile realized who her parents would be at Lom. Her father would befriend Barton and her mother would believe Jesa and Lillian to be her closest friends. She would share everything with them. Her parents would never find out about the Clown and the Bard; Emile could not even stretch her imagination enough to drop them there, to have them talking about life with Brody or the mechanics of Stealing with Dorian.

"What are you smiling about?" asked her mother curiously, watching Emile as she absently stayed fixed on them.

"A boy?" said Adelaide, who had returned and took a seat on the arm by Marshall's armchair.

Adelaide is the simplest puzzle there is, Emile studied her cousin's face. She could twist her heart around with a first grader's knowledge of her art. Its exact unquestioning quality imprinted itself onto her infant.

I pity that poor son of theirs, Emile thought. She saw all the iterations of his self along its destiny to grow up a pawn of a bigger game, unaware of what hovered just inches above him, unless he had any of Marshall to him. Marshall had a hidden side... but he was unmotivated, Emile realized. He was content with the life he had chosen, with having chosen a life less than what he was capable of.

Emile smiled secretively and shrugged, then shifted her gaze to Marshall.

"Marshall, did you ever read Emmannuelle?" she asked.

"What – no, not really," he glanced up, coming to in the conversation. "There are better books out there."

"Oh, like which?" she asked.

"I'll give you a list of my favorites in the morning. I think I'm being called to bed," he smiled as Adelaide tugged insistently on his arm to rise from the chair. The two bid Emile and her parents goodnight and went to the guest room.

Emile's mother patted the cushion beside her and Emile sat down and let her mother wrap her arms around her, burying her face into the hair now loose against the back of her neck. "I so rarely get to see my baby anymore, I forget you're practically a grown woman."

She softly stroked Emile's hair. The suspicion gripping her muscles and mind melted by the dying fire. The lack of pressure felt unnatural. Should she feel so relaxed? Had her body forgotten what it was like to be at ease? In her mother's arms, the presence of Lom grew smaller in her mind while the coziness of their living room grew bigger.

"I think I'll go to bed, too," her father stood up. Her mother dropped her arms to Emile's shoulders and then followed suit.

"And you, Emile?" asked her mother.

"I'll be up a little while," she said. In Lom, people would only be piling into the bar.

"Will you put out the fire before you go to sleep?" her mother said through a yawn. Emile nodded.

"Don't stay up too late, dear."

Wide awake, Emile remained watching the embers and reliving those scenes, missing the place with a strange pang.

After a few more restful days, Emile woke up on Sunday morning and took one last look around her clean, pretty bedroom. She could stay forever in the simple light... yet something pulled her back to Lom like a question left unanswered.

Her mother hugged her beside the train as if she might never see her again. Emile sensed her fear that, in a way, she never truly would. But underneath that she sensed resolve, told to her through her lingering hold.

"Emile, if you're not happy there, you don't have to go

back," she said. "You can go to school here."

This was her chance. She could escape the confusion, the sense that she was out of place. She knew a life at another school would be easy and comfortable, studying math and history and other dead subjects, but that she would only scratch the surface of the world's hidden mechanics. She would never peer deeper and she would never receive her certificate stating that she knew all of these truths, a certificate meaning nothing to the world but which she would hold inside herself.

"I want to go back," she said. Her mother's eyes grew saddened, but she nodded and let her board.

The train bounded for the darkening sky. Emile pressed, curled, against her window next to an overweight, suited man in a crowded compartment full of other men and women wearing business suits and toting briefcases, checking their watches and swaying with the train's stop and go as it made its usual stops. They looked like the last place they would go was the place she was going. She was the only child, but nobody paid her a glance. She daydreamed about Lom, and with a jolt saw Godfrey sitting in the one empty compartment corner, the little bells on his hat jingling while the train bumped on and he looking up from the floor and laughing at their anxious fidgeting while taking swigs from his flask.

His last words echoed in her mind: "*take care to return.*"

Panic shot through her. What if she *couldn't* return? She didn't know the way there. She had arrived by a mistaken train. This train so far showed no signs of heading back that way.

Emile anxiously watched out her window as they approached a fork: the rails split off right curving widely into bright, hilly countryside, or they veered left into a straight, deep dive toward piercing thin spires that she recognized. She clung to the ledge with frayed nerves while the people in her compartment read with blithe unconcern, as if nothing imminent was happening. They didn't see that an entire world hung in the balance of a hairpin turn! What if they simply bypassed the elusive door into Lom and rode on as if it never existed?

The train ground to a halt before the fork, and a mass exodus emptied the overly bright compartments, lifting the floor several centimeters from the released weight as only Emile and a few others remained. When the train started again, it tilted smoothly left and rode away from the sunny hills until twilight swallowed them. Emile breathed a sigh of relief and leaned back in her seat.

The castle was empty as on the first night she'd arrived, but this time Emile made for her refuge and penned a letter to the friend she had gratefully returned to:

Dear Wanderer,

Somehow, miraculously, I came back! I do not know how I got here in the first place and I worried the same accident would not happen again. I'll confess, part of me is happy to be back!

At home I found the simple life I've longed for so long, but I turned it away! I had the chance to remain there, to give up this confusion, but I didn't. Something called me back here. I can feel a new part inside me now that wants more than the life I grew up with. It's the part that's became a constant observer, a mistruster, a seeker of the underside, the part that never rests. I used to want peace and stability, but I've become engulfed by a kind of fire. I've outgrown my old village, too small to contain this new thing.

Yet I'm ever a stranger here. I live among them, but I ever will be one of them. The odd thing is that feeling out of place has become what's familiar, and anything calmer makes me uneasy. This is not the resting place of my heart... but, somehow, it is comforting to return to it! Where is my true home? What are my values? Who do I belong with? I no longer have answers to any of these questions. All I know is I am not the same as when I started here. I can no longer "just see", but see that the world is full of doors which most people overlook.

I think the true reason why I feel out of place is that I cannot reconcile the people. Godfrey and Jacqueline are so unbridled, so unabashed, so free... and I am always restrained, always holding myself back and thinking about what everyone else is thinking. Am I so inhibited because *I'm not home? I feel certain that if I found the way to you I would find what is crucial. Your presence still pulls me and I can always feel you on the other side of the door, just beyond my reach. Could the reason I returned not be to find* you? *I believe it is, and as long as I'm here I will try.*

Emile emerged from the empty library and headed to her room among the silent halls when a bone-piercing roar ripped through the air.

"EMILE!" Godfrey's voice thundered, shaking the paintings on the wall. "GET IN HERE, *NOW*!"

Feet frozen but the rest of her shaking, Emile collected herself and turned back to Godfrey's office.

He stood at his desk, rage emanating from his heart and filling each inch of the little room, never looking more intimidating than with his face so livid. Every ounce of his usual joviality was channeled into fury.

"*What have you done!?*" he yelled, slamming the table with his palm.

"Nothing!" she cried, confused.

"Don't pretend!" he roared.

She sputtered, "I remembered the lessons! I – I applied what we learned here at home! I proved I could manipulate and lie, I earned points – "

"*You manipulated your family!* Rather than face your classmates you chose soft targets who would never hurt you to show off a cunning you don't really possess! You're a weakling and a coward!" he sprayed her with spit as his face pulsed with blood. "Not only have you earned zero points, but you've *failed* Discrimination! *Strike one!*"

"Discrimination!? That was never on the list!" Emile objected.

"*What* list?"

"The one *you* gave – !"

"*And who am I*?" his voice overpowered.

"You're – !"

"*A man!* I'm just a man!" he finished, something desperate, almost pleading, in his tone now. He took shallow breaths, visibly trying to calm himself. "I could kick you out of my school right now if it weren't for the goodness of my heart!"

"Don't bother, I'll leave myself!" Emile exclaimed behind her tears.

She stormed to her room and grabbed her bags, sitting still packed by her bed, letting them bang all along the stone floor to the main hall. *It was a mistake to come back,* she decided. No matter how she stepped, it was wrong. Fifty feet now separated her from the freedom she should have taken months ago.

Someone was standing in the shadows, watching, but it wasn't Godfrey. It was Jacqueline, her figure framed in the archway with an air of preternatural calm.

"Emile, what are you doing?" she asked, even though it was perfectly clear what Emile was doing.

"I'm going home," Emile said, unable to conceal her

distress.

"Why?" Jacqueline's tone didn't change.

"I don't belong here."

"Why do you believe that?"

"You *know* why!" Emile lashed. "Just that! You *know* but pretend you don't because you're two-faced, and you teach us to be the same! You create a world that makes us form strategic alliances rather than friendships. I'm not that way and I don't want to be! I want to trust people, to be free – but you – here – you can't do that!"

"Your mother never mentioned that she went to school here?" Jacqueline asked after a pause.

"I don't believe you," Emile said, momentarily speechless. "She has a photo of her graduating class from Alvarus."

"That's because she left after two weeks. She never received her certificate."

"Then it only makes sense I follow her footsteps."

"Does it? Yes, you are like your mother. You're kind, unassuming, naïve. But you are stronger than she is; you adapt; you are curious; you want to know the other side," Jacqueline said.

"But if Godfrey himself told me I'm not Lom's kind – how

could I have a place here? He said on the first night I stumbled into the bar that there are two kinds of people, those who open their eyes to see and those who close them. Everyone here has their eyes wide open, but now I know what I'm the other kind," said Emile.

"Godfrey is an idiot," Jacqueline's voice turned sharp and cold like a knife dropped to the floor. "There aren't two types of people, there are two types of seeing, and you need both," she said. "Our students are always free to leave," she gestured to the door, "but I think you know that if you walk out now, you will not be able to return."

Emile stood for a minute, breathing, saying nothing, then let her bags fall to the floor.

"You can join your classmates for dinner," Jacqueline said with satisfaction and walked away, leaving Emile alone by the front door.

For the next several weeks, life at Lom resumed as if it had never been broken. There was no discussion of their weekend away, either by the students or the teachers. When Emile saw Lillian and Dorian, Jesa and Max, she couldn't imagine them outside of Lom; it seemed the only place they could exist. They proceeded smoothly with their classes and continued their outings to the bar until Godfrey abruptly broke the spell once again, gathering them all one Saturday morning at breakfast.

"We are starting a game today," he announced. "It is called 'Flash Forward'."

He handed each of them a heavy hard. Lillian leaped with delight when she read hers. In grand, swirling letters read the word "QUEEN" above a red dot in the center of a castle. It was the sun bursting full force into her world and scattering the clouds of her self-doubt, leaving clear blue skies that blared with triumphant trumpet notes. She knew now for certain that she would become who she always wanted to be.

Emile read her own. "simple," it said in plain letters. There was a castle in the middle like Lillian's, but it was empty, and a little red dot was outside it altogether in the uppermost corner.

Dorian, like Lillian, was pleased with his. "ORCHESTRATOR," it read in prominent bold letters. A red dot sat above the castle in the center of a tower, and right above it was a set of closed curtains. He had achieved, as had Lillian, his true place. He leaned back contentedly and casually flicked his card as he basked in the glory of his position until something caught his eye. On the other side of his card in small print on the very bottom was written the word, "heart."

"What is this?" he asked.

Nobody answered him.

They took to their roles that very morning. Everyone except Emile remained in the castle, but most followed their red dots back to their rooms as if it were an ordinary Saturday. There, they waited for something to happen.

Emile packed a bag and paused at the door to watch a plot already too dense to cut cleanly unfold in the center among the main players, before she turned her back on it for a final time. There was a wood around the castle, on the opposite side from town, leading into a large forest between them and the next town over. Emile went in that direction, trekking through the trees alone for many more hours after the castle and its noise faded, after the town was a memory but the memories of her old life did not take their place either and something new opened up. Something she had not yet found before but of which she felt confident. When the sun had descended midway, she found a remote cabin on a flattened clearing. It was sparse but beautiful, furnished with everything she needed. Instead of feeling alone felt she had arrived at a place that at once became home. Flash Forward's intent became obvious to her at once: it showed the clear road to her inevitable exit from the game.

Away from the castle, she returned to herself. She

breathed easy, as easy as she had in her mother's arms, but now not in the arms of her caretaker but rather the air and the leaves, the sun and the shade, the ground beneath her bare feet and the rhythm of the world. She rediscovered the woods and watched the rays play between yellow leaves in a world of gold. Here there was no duplicity, no childishness. The concerns of the world below let go of her as her days in this new life unfolded.

Godfrey had not given her this card for nothing; he knew her, and so he gave her a glimpse into a future she would forget once the game ended and not find again until it met her in the course of her life. But she had a taste of it now, of a life beyond Lom, having nothing to do with the school's curriculum or the world it belonged to.

Emile made preparations for the night as twilight approached, savoring the last plays the light made upon the bark as she searched for kindling when a light rustling made her jump. A figure fought through the forest brush toward her cabin, revealing itself after a few tense moments to be Dorian. He looked a great deal older and notches more smug, as if he'd aged many years since the start of Flash Forward. It took her a few moments to register him.

"What are you doing here?" she asked.

"Following my card," he said as if he didn't believe it

himself. Beneath his plastered on conceit he wore a look of confusion, unsure of why he had left a life as king to come to a lonely cabin far away.

"I'm supposed to find something," he said, his eyebrows knit together while he scanned the leafy ground.

"What?" Emile asked.

"I don't know, something small. It's probably under all these damn leaves," he kicked crackling clumps of them frustratedly, but it was as futile as diving for a gem in the ocean.

"What are *you* doing?" he asked to deflect her attention from his failing quest.

"Making a fire," said Emile as she continued to gather.

"You know how to do that?"

"Of course. You don't?"

"I've done it before," he said.

"Well, if you see any dry twigs along the way, pick them up for me," said Emile as they carried on their separate searches. But soon Dorian's search for his something melted into the search for kindling, which came far easier here, and he forgot about the something unexplained he was supposed to be looking for.

Together they built a fire, slowly stoking it as they sat around talking and laughing for hours into the safe kind of darkness that fell around them,

"Don't you ever miss it down there?" he asked her.

"No. I never did feel like I belonged. So I left, and now I'm happier here," said Emile.

"But you're alone," said Dorian.

"Castle life is too complicated for someone as simple as me," she joked.

"The stories I could tell," he sighed.

"I'm sure as Orchestrator you have the most complicated stories of all. It's a hard role."

"You just need to have people on your side. Like Barton? He lives to serve me. I appointed him Speaker; it makes him feel important, and that's all he really wants. That's the trick, knowing what people really want and what they fear. If you know that, you can manipulate anyone."

"Even the Queen?"

"Lillian is smart and always knows how to act, but what she desperately wants is Jacqueline's ever affirmed approval. Her other greatest fear is being out of the loop, and a Queen... well, nobody wants to tell her the truth. So we're best friends."

"Whatever happened to Jesa? I thought she was her best friend?" asked Emile.

"Jesa's perceptive and sly and she knows how to scheme, but she's not nearly as observant as Lillian and she's not a leader. She'll follow whoever has power. There's a jealous streak in her and Lillian's best-friendship-forever. I just pull on that string when I need something, whip up some drama around one, and the other is putty in my hands. She pulls on the string *for* me. Others are trickier – like Max. You have to pretend he *has* no fears. ... Once you figure it all out it's easy," but his face looked weary by the fire despite his nonchalance.

"It must take its toll," said Emile.

"Place hasn't changed. You *always* have to watch your back down there. It makes you hardened, you know?"

"I do. The first time I can really trust you is miles away from it," said Emile.

"Has nothing to do with distance. It's because you're not part of it anymore. At Lom, I wouldn't have trusted myself if I were you. *Especially* if I were you," he grinned, echoing their first meeting. "A funny thing about it is how it sneaks up on you. You don't notice how much it takes over. Then one day you realize you're never not playing the game," Dorian said."Out here it seems almost not worth it."

"It's not," said Emile.

"There are times I think I shouldn't bother anymore," Dorian admitted. "It means I need a break from reality."

"What reality?" asked Emile. "This isn't reality? There *are* people who understood that life is better for all of us if we look out for each other. Was it not like that where you grew up?"

"It was. And it was nice. But Trient has, like, ten people. If one person manipulates, the nine find out and he's screwed. The more people you get, the more you can hide. And I'll tell you, not everyone understands that it's better, and some people *do* understand but then use it! You offer them that kind of sincerity and they smile and pretend to agree, just waiting for the first second they get to crush that pure little world you hold up and take the gold in it. It's for them we learn to be watchful."

"Until we've become them," said Emile. "Then they've won. They've made us destroy what we were trying to preserve."

"I wish it could be another way," Dorian sighed, watching the fire cackle.

"It *can*! You're the biggest player in the game! If you

changed, everyone else would."

"Most people aren't you. They can't just make themselves stop," he smiled. "Besides, I'm too good at manipulating people. And the truth is, I'd get bored if everything was so simple. Though I do see the appeal of being a hermit. This must be the first moment in months I've truly relaxed."

"It's been nice talking to you outside the game," said Emile.

"I'm surprised you remembered how to talk to people," Dorian grinned. Emile poked him with a stick.

"I wish there was some compromise," he said minutes later. "A way to live there but escape to a place like this sometimes."

"Like a tunnel between here and the castle?"

"One only you and I know about. It'd be perfect. You could sneak in when you get lonely and I could sneak out when I need a break," he said.

"That's how we beat the game," said Emile.

"Two orchestrators from the cabin having the best of both worlds," he smiled.

"Just two simple cabin people with a hidden underground complex," she said.

They shook hands.

"How did you find this place?" he asked.

"I followed my card. How did *you* find it? Your card placed you above the castle."

Dorian showed her his card and flipped it to the other side.

"I don't know what this means," he said. For the first time, Emile heard vulnerability in his voice. He, who had always been so sure of himself, now followed "heart" to the middle of a cabin that returned him to a way he had long ago turned his back on.

He poked the fire excessively with a stick and they sat in silence for a long while before Dorian stood up.

"Well, the other side calls," he said, flipping his card back over to the castle.

"You don't have to go back there if you don't want to, you know," said Emile.

"'Heart' is only part of my card, and the smallest. And I didn't find it, anyway," he picked up the last firewood he'd collected and threw it into the flames, where it brightened them instantly but for a few seconds.

"Don't you think," Emile began in a small voice, but one

full of conviction," – didn't the thought occur to you – that *this* is what you came here looking for? Proof that there really is another way? That you don't always have to watch your back?"

"If I don't follow the card I'll lose," he said.

"Lose *what*? Another of Godfrey's games? Wouldn't you rather have a life that makes you happy over a game?"

"Life *is* a game, Emile, and I want to play."

Emile looked at him disbelievingly. "I don't get you. You hate it, yet you go back on your own. I think a part of you hates it, but a bigger part of you still loves the thrill you get from running the show. You feed off your own misery! Don't you see where this leads for you? Do you think if you keep playing you won't grow more tired?"

"What's the solution, then? To stay in the woods forever? You have everything you need here, don't you? Except the one thing you really want, which is to be a part of everyone else," Dorian threw back at her.

"I *do* want to be a part, but not of what goes on there. Didn't you hear yourself? You don't have a single friend in that life!"

"And I'm not fool enough to keep waiting for a change. You live in a world full of people, Emile, not just a world full of you." Then he added, "Well, I guess *you* do."

With that, he turned around and walked out of the clearing, swallowed up by the black forest. Emile knew without having to see that he was going to the Clown and the Bard.

The next morning, everyone returned to the castle. Flash Forward was over. They handed their cards over to Godfrey, who tore them up into pieces and threw them out of the tower window in the Foolishness classroom.

"Class dismissed," he waved them out. "Except you, Emile."

Emile held back, expecting to be asked about her time away from the castle in Flash Forward. Godfrey was sitting across his desk with his hands folded wearing a neutral expression and a bared head, his hat resting next to him. A piece of paper and a pen lay on the desk in front of him.

"It is time for your Evaluation," he said calmly.

It caught Emile off guard. "Me? Why? What about everyone else?"

"Everybody reaches their time. Yours is now."

"But – this isn't fair – you *want* me out! That's why – !"

"Now now, what makes you think you've failed?"

"I'm still in the middle, I'm working on – "

"Emile, you know the rules," he said with disappointment.

"No I don't! There *are* no rules!"

"That's one pass, very good," he marked a check off on the paper with satisfaction. "Let's see how you fared everywhere else." He cleared his throat.

"Discrimination you've already failed. Strike one," he made a big cross across the word.

"Drinking – improving," he acknowledged grudgingly, checking the paper. "Stealing – you've defended yourself, but barely any progress. You're too nice!" he chastised.

"Body Language – fine. Sensuality – fine as well," he said grudgingly again. "These are *almost* failing grades, by the way. I've never had such a hapless student scrape by."

"Lying and Manipulation – *failed*," he exclaimed with relish, drawing another prominent 'X' over the words. "Strike two."

"Proper Cooking and Cleaning – ninety-seven percent."

Emile flushed with pride in spite of herself.

"Driving Down Dangerous Roads – too much fear! It took you forever and you never truly let yourself go."

"And last but not least, Foolishness," he paused for

dramatic effect. "You gave away your last coins and took yourself out of the game in Stealing to merely prove some sort of point. You will have left a comfortable castle to become a hermit in a primitive cabin by yourself in the woods. You gave up the chance to be a successful student in a normal school where you would perfectly fit in to return to a place where you struggle and do not belong for a certificate you do not even care about and which nobody in the world will acknowledge. You are not the biggest Fool, but I think we can all agree that you are very, very foolish," he checked the paper with pride.

"That's only two classes. So I get my certificate!" the words felt odd on her tongue as news of the unexpected victory broke over her. Was that it? Was her time there over?

"Wrong!" Godfrey cried. "Anything less than one hundred percent in Proper Cooking and Cleaning is a failing grade. You know the rule – three courses and you're expelled! Get your things and leave the castle by nightfall. You are no longer a student of Lom."

"But – Where do I go? I have no money – "

"My advice? Anywhere out of my sight," Godfrey said, packing the record up neatly with his other papers and putting away the pen. "Perhaps you should've thought of that *before* you so determinedly put fifty percent into all your classes."

"Wait – please – " Emile pleaded as he got up and walked out. "Can I have another chance? I'll learn to manipulate, I'll learn to steal!"

"You had a chance every day, and now that you're all out of them you want to apply yourself at last?"

She looked searchingly at his face to draw water from the empty well of his inscrutable eyes. They may have held sorrow or they may have held joy. They may have held utter indifference.

"I wouldn't be much of a leader if I went back on my word, would I? I suggest packing your bags sooner rather than later. After dark you won't be able to get into your room. Oh, and if I catch you sleeping in my bar again, I'll be the one to escort you out," he left, leaving her in the Foolishness tower.

The sun was falling over the trees beyond the window, weak enough that she could stare at it. Long summer shadows lay over the thick grass upon the grounds. The few remaining hours before her expulsion were beautiful and warm; the world was bathed in golden light.

Would everybody have gotten word by now? What would she do if they asked her why Godfrey had held her back? Emile followed him out of the tower but did not head for her room as she passed other students on their way to dinner and avoided catching their eyes. She was no longer one of them. She had no place here. She was walking through a stranger's house on her way to a world no less hostile to her; it was Godfrey's world beyond the grounds, too.

This was no end to his grasp; she was never more in it! Now she was a beggar in his kingdom and when night fell, it would be her first night utterly alone! She had nobody, for everybody she knew was part of the game of Lom.

Dear Wanderer,

This is my last letter to you. My greatest fear has at last come to pass: I've been kicked out of school and I have nowhere to go. I have no money and no friends in this strange town where I'm left to wander like a pariah. If only I had put aside my endless doubting and done what I needed to do to survive! If only I had accepted this town for what it is and stopped wishing it was something else! I'm out of chances now. I belong to nothing. You are the only hope I have left. If I don't find you again, I don't know what I'll do. I fear I'll remain forever lost! Please come and find me. Please let me find you again.

Your Friend,

Emile

She headed swiftly to the kitchens, stealing a few precious minutes to rifle through utensils for anything that might pry open a door. With a heavy ladle in one hand and the letter in the other, she skirted to the library past several curious stares, opening the hatch and moving as quickly as she could through the tunnel.

Emile beat her fists against the wooden door pressed firmly into the dirt around it, but as always it was to no avail. It was dark on the other side, not yet nightfall.

"Open the door! Please!" she cried, banging her fists again, then trying to pry it open with the ladle. She didn't gain an inch.

In the middle of her banging, dim light began to glow and seep through the cracks. She stopped, pressed her ear, then resumed banging louder.

"OPEN THE DOOR! *PLEASE!* OPEN!"

The light was the only change. The silence remained. Her remaining time could be counted in minutes. Putting all of her hope into the last letter, she mouthed a wish and slid it under the door. She dropped the ladle and ran back to the library.

A cerulean sky hosted the first rising stars past the latticed windows in the hallway. Godfrey would be making his way to the bar soon.

The library door shut with a soft thud behind her. Jolted, Emile tried to open it again, rattled the knob, but it stayed closed. The castle was closing itself to her. Every hallway door was shut. So was the door to the kitchens, the door to the dorms. She didn't run into a soul in the castle, but occasionally she thought she saw a tall shadow on the far side of a hall – a teacher, she thought – and hid in a corner or behind a pillar until the person passed. If the castle was kicking her out, it was under Godfrey's orders. They would be, too.

Emile opened the front door, overlooking the town in a hazy summer's night framed by trees that rustled like a deep teal ocean in twilight.

"Emile?" said a curious, uncertain voice.

Barton, the only person in the castle, approached her from the direction of the kitchens juar she took her final steps there. He looked as lost as ever. His search for liquor bottles was continuous, and he had come up empty since the first week.

"Are you leaving?" he asked curiously.

The summer breeze blew pleasantly through the door.

"Evaluations started, didn't they? I'm so worried I'll fail," he said without her answer. He looked down at the checkered stone floor while the night stood open to him.

"Barton, go to the bar tonight," she said.

He blinked. "The bar isn't real, Emile."

"Do you have a pen?"

With the one he confusedly gave her, she roughly outlined a route to the Clown and the Bard from the castle on his arm.

"If you don't know which door it is, try them all. The right one will open easily. Go there tonight once it's fully dark. Dorian, Lillian, Jesa, Max, all the teachers will be there. They're the only ones who know. And me."

"Thank you, Emile," he said, his open mouth turning slowly into a smile. She felt a tide rising slowly behind her as she walked out of the school.

She ambled about town, unsure of where she was going. Nowhere to turn to and not a coin in her pockets. As she wrung her hands in desperation, she saw among the several people moving leisurely about one moving much faster: a small figure, a little girl, was running along the dark street ahead, visible by a lamp swinging in her hand. Emile broke into a run, getting close enough to glimpse the very unruly black hair and celestial nightgown she had been seeking for months. Her heart leaped with excitement.

Emile followed her swift, steady pace across town, following her through tiny alleyways and around turns and even over fences, stretching her hand out to grab the nightgown, until without notice she followed the girl through a doorway straight into, to her horror, the Clown and the Bard.

Instinct almost spun her around, but curiosity pulled her on through the thick Friday crowd. The girl was somewhere in here, she distinctly, certainly knew it. She and her little light had been swallowed by the drunken bodies, and not a flicker shone through the gaps between them.

Emile carefully wove around, searching, dodging momentary glances from some of the teachers. Pair by pair, the eyes of the many laughing regulars latched onto her presence in the dim lamplight. Emile shot for the bar, to her only chance of safety hiding behind the wall of a large man.

"Brody, I need your help," she panted. "Please, hide me upstairs for a while. I'll work for you, stock the bar, whatever you need – I just need a place to stay."

"I'll have to check with Godfrey, he does the hiring," Brody said, taken by surprise.

"No!" Emile threw a frantic glance back into the crowd behind her. She knew Godfrey was in the middle of it. "He won't let you. He already kicked me out of the school."

"It's *you*?" realization spread over Brody's face. "I knew it was someone, the only time Godfrey ever forgets his hat is when he kicks out a student. It weighs on his heart."

At that very moment, Godfrey's roaring laugh rode the crest of a noisy wave that erupted behind them. It sounded as if they had just done a toast.

"He puts on a brave face," Brody said. Emile threw an anxious glance back and saw that Brody was right about one thing: the tip of the jester's hat and the habitual jingling of bells was missing from the cacophony. She only saw the top of Godfrey's bare brown head buried among necks and faces, among whose were Dorian's and Lillian's.

"I'm sorry, Emile, I wish I could help. I'm under Godfrey's orders," Brody said with a pained look.

What had made her believe he would help her? Brody was friendly, but he wasn't her friend. She had forgotten. This was why she had failed. The fact remained that he was a member of this world, and his loyalty was to it and its people.

Godfrey's voice grew louder and clearer as he moved through the crowd to get another drink. Emile bolted, running behind the throng to keep out of his view, snaking between tables and catching confused stares.

"Barton!?" she heard Lillian's cry of disbelief as she ran past her classmates, felt the shockwave rip through the tiny space as Dorian dropped his glass onto the floor. The next moment, he and Max pulled Barton into their circle with smiles and led him to the bar for his first shot.

Emile ran on, glancing back at the bar and locking eyes with Brody right as he looked up from an exchange with a hidden figure on the other side of the counter. A wave surged and poised itself before her. Emile flew down the stairs, flung open the bathroom. No; he would break it down. She was in Godfrey's own bar. The wanderer had led her into a trap.

As soon as she thought this, a familiar light bobbed out from behind a box in a dimly lit storage area as the tiny girl ran around them.

"Wait!" Emile cried to the back ever to her. The girl did not wait. She gave no sign of hearing Emile. She ran deeper into the basement with Emile at her heels bumping into boxes, barrels, and old furniture while keeping the faint cloth stars in her gaze. The wanderer turned behind a stack of boxes and disappeared into the air.

She had turned into dead end, a box wall to her right and the stone wall to her left. A scuffed wooden floor lay beneath, but directly below her feet she traced a smallish hatch, not unlike the one in the library, complete with an etching of a lantern and a star. She opened it easily and shut it behind her just as footfalls thundered into the room.

She had found her home! She had reached the wanderer from the other side! The cellar was wider than the tunnel at the school, lit by a single lamp by the door. Barrels stood stacked against the wall for a short stretch until the cellar grew longer, narrower, and darker. The wanderer was absent. At the end, barely seen in the light, was yet another small door.

Her only true smile at Lom broke across her face. At last, she had found the home she had sought for so long, buried in the hidden center of this world. Its existence was not even a myth. It was entirely unknown to the students, even the insiders who prided themselves on knowing everything about Lom. Even Godfrey himself might not know it. But she, Emile, had found it. She had found the very heart.

The little door had merely a latch to slide open, nothing more. She peered through its cut into darkness. Why would the wanderer be sitting in darkness? Something rustled under her feet as she reached for the latch. Emile was standing on paper. There on the ground, blending into the dirt, lay a sheaf of letters in a pile like a ragged doormat. In the faintest light Emile made out her own handwriting. She reread some of her own earlier thoughts. They were still creased in the places where she had folded them as she carried them clandestinely around the school, and the ones that had been folded completely – the most private – remained that way still.

She pulled open the door and faced the tunnel she had so often come down from the other side. Leaving her letters and the Clown and the Bard behind, she stepped through and ran up to the castle, up the stone steps into the library, up through the empty halls all the way to the Foolishness classroom whose door stood open as she'd left it that afternoon. Godfrey's hat still sat on his desk.

She grabbed the hat and sprinted back out, back into town, the jingling bells a messenger's song, heading not to the Clown and the Bard but to the train station.

It was empty save for a lone employee sitting behind a glass counter, wearing the surly expression of one for whom nothing exciting has happened in too long.

"I need a ticket for the next train to Prague," Emile said breathlessly. Without a word or a look at her the attendant penned in her ticket.

"I don't have money," she said without reading the ticket, "but I have something else."

She held up the dirty hat. The man's face shed decades off its pasty front as if the long years of waiting behind this counter had revealed their purpose at last, and he gazed upon the faded felt as upon a treasure, fantasies dancing in his widened eyes as the chance to be king dangled before the plexiglass. He looked up at Emile with a mixture of awe and confusion, wondering why she herself hadn't taken the open throne. But Emile only longed to go home.

Fumbling, he hastily ripped off the ticket and unlocked the window to make the trade.

"Stop!" yelled a voice behind them, reverberating among the marble pillars.

Godfrey stood in the middle of the station, drunk with his head bared under the light. In one hand he held all of Emile's letters. He held them up, a grin spreading.

"Weakness for weakness," he offered.

He came into sharp view as light behind them filled the empty hall and a train whistle bounced off the columns. The next train to Prague had arrived.

"Please," Godfrey said, his voice cracking. He opened the most tightly folded letter, dramatically cleared his throat, and read, "*Sometimes I think I see a part of him that nobody else does, a part he's forced to hide in our sicks games. There have been brief moments when I've felt that Dorian and I have truly connected and where I even trusted him, but more importantly, where he trusted me. But the next day, it's as if it never happened. He reverts to being the Dorian everyone sees and I feel like a fool once again for having listened to what my heart said... or, maybe, what my heart simply* wanted...."

The train station worker laughed along with Godfrey as Godfrey rifled for more.

"I don't care," said Emile. "Show everyone." Just as a hole into this strange world had appeared before her, so did a gateway now materialize behind.

"You beat me, Emile. You stole my most prized possession and manipulated me into making a deal. And for that, you have earned a second chance," he was unable to hide the plea in his voice. He brandished the letters, his face contorted with worry, and for the first time, with the glaring light from the train falling upon it, Emile glimpsed the many lines in it.

She stood on the seam of worlds, still clutching the jester's hat and facing a second chance to earn the most prized treasure of a nonexistent world.

But a hand was pushing her back; it was time to go. She

shook her head and with a last pitying look at Godfrey turned around and boarded the train to Prague.

Part II

It was quiet inside for how many people had crammed into the compartment. Most paid no mind to the little town they had paused at, a town barely enough to merit a blip on the map and probably not worth sparing a glance up for.

The instant Emile stepped in, the world of Lom faded behind her, so quickly that she giggled at the sound of its name, a few paces in turned it into a ghostly realm, and the last few threads had seconds more to cling on until the moving train snapped them.

Larger bodies jostled her from all sides and one grabbed at the back of her shirt, pulling, until it was her arm they held.

The pasty man so sweaty even the hairs on his arm lay flat on his skin was Godfrey. "Please, Emile. Make this trade with me," he pleaded in something of a mumble under hair plastered flat to his forehead. He'd jumped from the platform, planted both feet on the train. Emile stared at the man in shock, in his torn and dirty tunic, shorter than most of the men around him, stouter than many, his eyes roving around as if he hadn't stepped onto a train in years.

"You don't understand," he rasped. His face was chubbier than she remembered. Was this the man who would sleep late into the morning and command his own school come Monday?

"You don't understand," he repeated, slurring slightly but trying to impress something upon her. "But you could."

A whistle signaled seconds until departure. The last few people boarding the train jostled him as they rushed aboard; no one seemed to recognize him. Godfrey maintained his pleading look at Emile, who realized she was still clutching the jester's hat. Taking Godfrey's hand, she jumped off the train with him. The compartment closed instantly behind them and the train sped on, taking its blinding light along.

"Thank you, Emile," Godfrey said, putting his hat back on and exchanging Emile her stack of letters. She wrapped them into a neat tube, and when they reached the castle, she went back to her room and tucked them away into a suitcase.

Emile rejoined life at Lom as if little had changed. Exteriorly, little had. The intrigues unfolded further; new lessons were introduced; their relationships remained relatively unchanged. The only real difference was that Barton now knew of the Clown and the Bard. But the insiders quickly patched this hole to where it was under control: they made it very clear that should Barton tell anyone else about the bar, they would fail him instantly.

Emile no longer went to the library or wrote to the wanderer. The tunnel remained a secret with her, still a refuge from castle life, but one she seldom took, preferring to wander the grounds instead. She floated through the classes, deflecting smoothly in all of her interactions. Under the play, she carried the unshakeable sense that she was moving against her destiny. She felt she should not be there. She had stood at a crossroads with a clear light home, but she had chosen the other way for a look on a man's face that broke wide open her explanation of him. It was a fluke in the equation that kept her there; she could remain in Lom because her forbidden action had been canceled by Godfrey's own.

Occasionally she passed Gaunt in the halls and shared a momentary understanding; was she, too, becoming a ghost? Was she fated to carve a home in a world where she didn't belong?

Summer had begun its descent. The forest was molting one beauty for another, its deep, buoyant greens bound up in the hot months' trials giving way to orange and yellow with streaks of red. A rustle like tambourines filled the air as the curling edges shook in the breeze.

One morning a rumor circulated that a musician was passing through town. A nomad, unlikely to stay long. The mention spiked Emile's fascination, and she found herself thinking he might want to know about the cabin in the woods.

"He is only here for the day," Godfrey addressed it at lunch, "and he's offered to hold a concert for us this afternoon. It will be a treat for you all, a true experience."

Godfrey promptly canceled their afternoon classes and gathered them in a study, where they formed a circle on the old Persian rug.

"Dorian, escort him in," Godfrey said. Dorian looked surprised at being chosen for this role, but did as Godfrey ordered and returned a minute later with a tall, thin man of attractive physique and a youthful face sculpted with a straight nose and a chin hidden in an untrimmed beard. Everything about him was loose, what lent him his charm. Rich brown curls swung by his graceful neck just over the seam of an off-white linen shirt hanging from his broad shoulders and caught under his belt at his thin waist. The only meticulously crafted part on him was a brightly embroidered guitar strap pressed to his flat chest.

Emile lingered on the vision of them side by side: polar opposite, they sharpened each other's features and in that instant she loved both immensely. On the right stood Dorian, the image of Godfrey, square, alert, calculating, flat on the ground with his eyes on the world around him, fully aware of the labyrinth and his role in it; the half of the world opposite Emile. On the left stood the musician, relaxed and free, blind to the world's expectations, his gaze turned inward. He lived in the flourishing world within himself. For the first time, Emile felt something in this world beam her own spirit back to her. Then with a note of sadness she recalled that he was only passing through.

The musician's bright brown eyes barely looked over his audience as he took his place in the center of the rug and disappeared into the meticulous task of tuning his lute without glancing up once to see who he was playing for. He easily ignored the whispers that broke out around him.

His melodic tuning eased into playing. Folk melodies issued from the strings. Emile closed her eyes and lost herself in the music's landscape. Her heart leaped to hear a familiar tune from Locronan that pierced her mental fog like an arrow and brought her straight into the freedom and joy she had lived there, as really as if she were walking to the shore that very instant.

An invisible string jerked at her. Emile snapped open her eyes and discovered that she was the only one other than the musician who was lost in a reverie. The rest of the class watched him like guard dogs, studying his every detail with sharp and wary eyes. His unplanned movements were so unlike their every step. His manner fascinated them, but they stopped at the gate, unable to understand.

Never had the divide between two forking paths been clearer. The people of Lom were ever observant of the world around them, their eyes ever open to make sure nothing escaped their watch. They adjusted themselves to the winds like finely tuned weather vanes, playing upon each nuance. They opened their eyes to see; the musician closed them. He was the main and only character in his story. His problems were wrapped tightly around himself; other people – he did not even see them. The rules commanding the outside world, the townsfolk's everpresent concern, did not exist for him in his impervious bubble.

He packed up quickly when he finished and slipped out. Everyone in the hall jumped to deliberate what had just happened, but Emile went to walk the grounds to digest alone. As she came back around to the castle, she found the musician near the gate, saddling up a mule that stood apathetically by the castle wall with eyes half closed. He threw a sack filled with various possessions over its back and looked ready to set off.

"You played a chanson from Locronan," Emile said.

He turned to her, surprised. "Indeed. You know it?"

"I'm from Locronan."

"Ah! A beautiful village," he smiled.

"You've been there?"

"I've been all over. They have excellent music."

"What brought you here?" she asked him.

He shrugged. "A whim. I'm only passing through. I never stay."

"Where are you going now?"

"I don't know," he said lightly. "I'll end up somewhere."

His long waves swished across his face as he piled another bag onto the donkey with easy languor, but Emile had the distinct impression he was itching to leave as quickly as possible.

"You're the first musician to come through since I've been here," she said.

"It's not much of a place for musicians, is it? Different crowd," he validated Emile's own sentiments.

"They're sharp and observant. They notice everything."

"They have talent for little else," he derided. "Do you play music?"

"I play the lute as well."

He studied her. "Interesting. How did you end up here?"

"I think by accident."

"Then why do you stay?" he asked.

Emile considered it, trying to pinpoint the reason. "I'm too curious about a world that's foreign to me. Living in discomfort has made me stronger."

"But this isn't your place. You will never flourish."

"I don't know where my place is anymore," she said.

"Regardless, it won't hurt you to play your lute once in a while. Maybe you'll bring music back here."

With that, the musician carefully placed his lute onto his bags and seated himself onto his mule, waving to her and abandoning the castle grounds like a light breeze. At once the breath of fresh air that had floated into Emile's world was gone and she was plunged back into the stagnant pool where she'd swirled for months. She watched his figure grow smaller among the yellowing leaves without taking a backward glance at what it left behind. She felt more alone than ever.

On the edge of the grounds where the forest began, she found Dorian standing by himself, facing the trees. He appeared still and deep in thought.

"What are you doing out here?" Emile asked.

"Nothing," he said simply.

"The musician really affected you?"

Dorian nodded.

"Do you play music?" Emile asked.

"No. Do you?"

"I play the lute."

"So you're like the musician."

"I am," Emile answered without ambiguity.

They stood side by side, a clear line finally drawn between them.

Across it, Emile said, "You don't have to worry about sneaking out of the castle anymore. I found an escape: there's a tunnel from the library that goes to the Clown and the Bard. I thought you'd want to know."

"That's no escape. It's a shortcut," he said without breaking eye contact with the trees.

The tiny apparitions of Lillian and Jesa came running across the grounds toward them, excited and out of breath, their faces bright and their mouths ready to burst open with news.

"Come on! Something's happening at the Clown and the Bard! Everyone's down there!"

Jesa pulled on Dorian's arm as Lillian took Emile by the hand and pulled her away from the forest and into the town.

A cacophony met their senses. Upbeat, rapid fiddle music trilled through the air and the tables were crammed against the walls for a makeshift dance floor in the middle. Godfrey and Jacqueline danced while the audience clapped along. His hat was askew, his footfalls thudded like a great bear's against the stone floor; he sang throatily in a deep, raspy voice. Jacqueline's dress spun like a flimsy umbrella and her long hair whipped through the air. She looked happier and freer than Emile had ever seen her. But to her greatest shock, pressed up against the wall behind them sat none other than the musician, perched on a stool and nearly tearing his fiddle to shreds as his curls bounced rhythmically with his head in beat with the music.

His eyes were shut tight. His fingers moved faster than he could think. The dance floor rapidly filled with couples spinning each other to this raucous folk tune amid steady whistles and claps. Walls that had stood for months within Emile crumbled in confusion.

Emile felt a tap on her shoulder and turned around to Dorian's smiling face. She took his outstretched hand and he lead her into the crowd on the dance floor. With one hand laced and the other holding on, they twirled around in the drunken haze that blurred separate worlds together and let their elements run like paint into inexplicable colors. He pressed his forehead to hers as they spun in time to the music, nut out of time's passage. For the first instant, Emile questioned nothing. The song ended on a swift note. They stopped, breathless.

"Children!" Godfrey roared, embracing them with great sweeps of his arms and uniting them for a drink. After the three of them toasted, Godfrey ordered another round and raised his glass ceremoniously.

"A toast to Emile's earlier victory, long overdue," he raised his.

"You nearly broke the dam, bringing Barton in here," Dorian said.

"She almost upended the whole damn thing! Imagine! Giving the rank of Fool to a complete idiot!" but Godfrey smiled, for she didn't. They toasted Emile and Dorian disappeared back into the crowd. Godfrey remained with Emile and ordered them each a beer.

"Maybe if *you* taught Lying and Manipulation I wouldn't have been able to," said Emile.

"I don't have time to teach everything with a school and a bar to run. I know it doesn't look to you like I do much other than drink, but I'm a very busy man," he said.

"Then why don't you let someone else teach Foolishness?" asked Emile.

"I'll tell you a secret," he leaned in. "No one else is qualified to teach Foolishness."

"Not even Jacqueline?"

Godfrey threw back his head and laughed. "Jacqueline is the farthest thing from a Fool."

"Then teach her."

"One cannot be taught Foolishness by another," Godfrey said.

"How did you learn?"

A small smile spread across Godfrey's face. "Life made a Fool out of me."

"How?"

"It was many years ago, the details are hazy to me now,"

he waved it off, but Emile saw through. She imagined herself as Lillian, surveying the bar for that someone who knew the story. Gaunt knew, but he would never reveal. Brody was too young. One more person would know and be willing to share....

"Gunter!" Emile called. Gunter stumbled toward them, large and jolly drunk.

"Do you remember how Godfrey became a Fool?" she asked.

Gunter boomed with laughter. "Do I!" he patted his belly.

"I thought you would. You're one of Godfrey's oldest friends.

"I'm Godfrey's *oldest* friend. I've known him since well before he was the great man you see before you today," Gunter put his arm around his oldest friend.

"That must be a *very* long time, because Godfrey can't even remember the day he became a Fool," said Emile.

"The most important day of your life? Age must be getting to you," he turned to Godfrey. "We were young men, I was a few years out of school and Godfrey had just finished at Lom. He was ready to take over the world."

"Of course you were students here," Emile said to herself.

"You wouldn't have recognized it back then. Godfrey's made quite a few changes since he became headmaster."

"All for the better," Godfrey interjected. "I teach what you really need to know, not garbage everyone realizes years down the line was a waste of time."

"And to think, if you'd taken that scholarship the world might not be blessed with your tutelage," Gunter laughed. "A scholarship to one of the best universities and you turned it down! I'll never let it go!" he howled.

"Why?" Emile balked at Godfrey.

"That was the summer Jacqueline came to town," Gunter explained.

"You fell in love with her, didn't you?"

"He more than fell in love. He lost his head! Only problem was, Jacqueline was engaged to a much older, much richer lawyer who'd moved here to start a practice. Her parents were thrilled."

"So was he," Godfrey added drunken perspective. "The most beautiful girl in town, all the money in the world – what more could a man want?"

"She didn't love you back," Emile realized as an inkling of sympathy bloomed in her towards Godfrey.

Gunter laughed darkly. "She loved him back, alright. Every week she loved him back and every other week she ignored him in the streets like he didn't exist. It went on like that for a year."

"Why couldn't she just pick one?"

"You're so young, Emile. Haven't you been paying *any* attention in class?" Gunter asked.

"She barely passed Sensuality," Godfrey muttered.

"Jacqueline didn't know *what* she wanted," Gunter explained. "That was the problem."

But Godfrey's private grin revealed the moments that made him certain it was otherwise. For a second, Emile glimpsed the unspoken link that existed only for them, a vestige of the tender intimacy from the days when their bond had blossomed with chance, tired and slack now from the wear of stretch and misuse, but still made of gold that glinted over all other factors of the world when they glanced at each other across the room.

"She knew, she just couldn't listen to it," Godfrey said."Too much of her wanted what her parents wanted for her."

"You'd be surprised that her parents didn't want her with a poor troublemaker who had too much fun," Gunter chuckled.

"Parents don't have to live their children's choices," Godfrey said.

Gunter explained to Emile, "Jacqueline's mother was cruel and vain. She taught her how to go about love, so when Jackie found it she mangled it. No one taught Godfrey about love. When it found him, he did its bidding. That's what made him a Fool."

Godfrey raised his half emptied glass.

"Godfrey was dirt poor but smart, a favorite around town. People loved him. Everyone thought he had a bright future so it was to no one's surprise when he got a scholarship. A perfect shot to kick out and make a life for himself. But," Gunter sighed and put his arm around Godfrey, "our friend turned it down and stayed in town so he wouldn't lose Jacqueline. Thought he was this close to swaying her. He even took a job as her fiancee's assistant just to be closer to her. Worked day and night while the bastard coasted, struck dumb by what a hardworking lad he'd found. 'Course, eventually he realized what was going on – the last in town to catch on," Gunter chuckled. "As you might imagine, such an important man didn't like being taken for an idiot by a wily young boy. He was cruel. He started hinting he'd pay Godfey's way through school. Godfrey took the bait and worked even harder. He had no idea the man knew he was in love with her – by then it was plain to the blind. Godfrey thought he was about to win the lottery. The rest of us could see he was about to fall headfirst. The man was disgustingly pompous. You *wanted* Godfrey to pull one over him."

"So... you did, didn't you? That was how you learned everything?"

Godfrey merely kept smiling to himself.

"About a year and a half after Jacqueline had moved here, things were starting to quiet down between her and Godfrey. They barely saw each other. And the way she spoke to him in public – was as if she'd never met him. Broke his heart every time, but for some reason nobody can understand that gave him more resolve to keep trying. He got wind that a certain unique and very expensive necklace had captured her heart and that she'd declared it the necklace she would wear on her wedding day. Her fiancee made a big show of ignoring this, but Godfrey saw through his bluff. He knew he was going to surprise her with it. That's where he saw his chance. It cost almost everything he'd saved up. The look the attendant must've given him..." Gunter laughed.

As if she were there, the scene of a snowy winter evening unfolded before Emile. She watched a young, spry Godfrey with shining eyes and buoyant steps march through frozen streets now familiar to her carrying a shiny wrapped box under his arm. He slipped it into his coat pocket before he entered a stately house sagging with antique furniture to endure a painful dinner with a strikingly beautiful and vivacious young Jacqueline and an older, self-indulgent, but intimidatingly clever man.

"...And Madelyn's dog unraveled the entire sweater running around the field," Jacqueline said as her fiancee and Godfrey both chuckled. "He's so silly. He'll need another after how he's grown since summer."

"If she hasn't got an entire pound by then," her fiancee added. "I can't supply clothes for a hundred dogs."

"Don't say that. She won't," Jacqueline said.

"Your cousin isn't known for her good sense, dear."

Godfrey had remained half off his chair for the duration of dinner. A server took back dessert and they moved to sit by the fireplace. Godfrey began to visibly work up his courage, drinking scotch procured from a glass bottle entirely too quickly. She could see Jacqueline eying his motions as she delicately sipped hers in rhythm with her fiancee.

When he had drunk enough, Godfrey pulled the box from out of his jacket pocket and presented it to Jacqueline, keeping focused on her face. She looked speechlessly up at Godfrey, whose look made no effort to mask his intentions.

A tiny grin spread over her fiancee's face as he watched Godfrey, a warning sign that slipped past the entranced young lover.

"It was you, Godfrey?" he feigned surprise. "I couldn't believe it, when I went for the necklace it turned out somebody had bought it. I had a time making it up to you, dear," he told Jacqueline.

He pulled around a large box the size of a night stand. Perplexed, Jacqueline laid the necklace down gently and opened it to reveal a leather suitcase.

"Open it," said her fiancee.

Inside Jacqueline found a far tinier box and opened it to find a single shiny key.

"The lock is in France," he said. "Right by the water, on the edge of town."

Her jaw dropped. "But I thought you couldn't leave – !"

"We'll be near enough to Paris that I can work there."

"I can't believe....We're really going," she said breathlessly.

"We have Godfrey to thank for this chance. Thanks to all his hard work, things have moved faster than I thought and we'll manage fine now. Thank you, Godfrey, for making us both *so* happy" he nodded to the young man as he held

Jacqueline around her waist. Jacqueline averted Godfrey's eyes.

Godfrey left immediately, unable to force himself to sit through a moment more. He marched through the thickly falling snow, moving rapidly to stay numb within a swirling cocktail of heartbreak, humiliation, and disbelief.

He stopped a few blocks down and leaned against a building, no longer able to keep his pain at bay and addressing it with a rapid slew of possible plans while the snow covered his face. Over an hour he stood in the cold, his lips growing blue, until Jacqueline's fiancee suddenly walked under the lamp across the street without spotting Godfrey, a smug expression on his face visible from afar. Godfrey's blood boiled, realizing he was on his way for a few drinks. Godfrey mobilized and ran right back to their house.

A light in the master bedroom showed Jacqueline's silhouette. Deftly, Godfrey climbed up a frozen ladder to her window, freezing his fingers and slipping several times.

"What are you doing?" she hissed, pulling him in through her window. "If he sees you...."

"I doubt he will, I just passed him on his way to the bar. You're going to marry someone who leaves you on your birthday?"

"He went to get a bottle of wine," Jacqueline said.

"You don't believe that, do you?"

"What do you want?" she demanded.

"You don't want to do this. I saw it on your face at dinner. I can see it now!" Godfrey said. He reached out to touch her cheek and found it wet with tears. Her clothes lay disheveled on her bed, halfway packed. "Why are you making yourself do this?" he pleaded.

"I made a promise," she held up her hand and a ring glimmered in the room. "You don't go back on a promise when a bad feeling comes along."

"So this whole time – you and I – that was a distraction from bad feelings?" Godfrey withdrew.

"Of course not! You know that, you know I care for – I didn't plan on meeting you."

"Well you did."

"Godfrey, you don't understand... I never intended to build a life here. I can't stay here. This is a dead end. I've been planning to leave since I arrived."

"We don't have to stay here! We can go somewhere else," he seized on the chance.

"And what will we live on?" she asked softly.

"I won't let us starve," he defended.

"How? You don't have – "

"Because I gave it up for *you*!" he bristled with anger.

"What were you thinking with that necklace?" she burst out. "All your savings? How could you be such an idiot!?"

"Don't you see that I would give up *everything* for you?" Godfrey stood helpless to make her see. "What's another house to him? He already has five!"

"It isn't about the house. It's more complicated than that...."

"How?"

"We've built a world together. We have friends, family, history. Names we've picked out for children. We have a life planned out. You and I have feeling, but... that's it."

"So you love me?"

"Of course, I love you! Do you think I would've done any of this if I didn't love you?"

"Then why can't you be with me!"

"Because there's more to consider than love!" she cried, collapsing onto her bed. "It doesn't make sense. I have everything in this life, but you, a tiny grain outside it, mean as much as the whole thing!"

"What can I give you but everything intangible?" he sank glumly next to her.

"Don't be naïve," she moaned. "I never wanted to choose."

"It's fine," he said sadly, draping his arm resignedly around her. "You'll be happy on your island. You won't even miss me."

"Yes I will. My heart is breaking thinking this might be the last time I see you," she turned to her and he saw the tears forming in her eyes, almost big enough to start rolling down her cheeks. She buried herself into his chest and cried.

"This is always what you do," he hissed as he hugged her.

"What *I* do!?"

The front door unlocked without a sound some time later, but a very audible voice at the stairs called, "Jacqueline!"

Jacqueline jumped out of bed like a rabbit. Godfrey was too stupefied to comprehend. He rolled naked onto the foot of the bed as her fiancee walked in and ran at him, pulling him toward the window while Jacqueline pleaded with him to stop.

The calmness in her fiancee's face was unnerving. He seemed less angered by Jacqueline's betrayal and more annoyed by Godfrey's presence. He dragged him down the stairs by an arm and an ear to the front door and beyond, down the street, back to the bar from where he came, where he tossed him inside through the door and turned around.

"...And that was the night I met Godfrey," Gunter concluded, "forced to listen to the sad tale of a naked boy without a penny as he realized he'd given up his chance at a better life for a woman who blew him off for a richer man," Gunter finished. "Guess who of us was surprised? No one!"

"Jacqueline did what was smart. She's no Fool," Godfrey cut in rather hoarsely.

"He looked at that door all night. She never did show up, and he didn't see her for years after that night. They left that weekend, and a week later so did Godfrey. Sold his last things to scrape some money and took off. Nobody saw him or heard from him for years. What happened out there, no one knows, and it's probably best not to know," Gunter turned to his friend, "but he returned a changed man and opened up this bar. Shocked everyone who knew him. Godfrey hadn't been much of a drinker. *I* was the troubled one," Gunter smiled as Godfrey started on his next beer, then burped and leaned back, almost falling off of his stool. Emile followed his unfocused gaze to the table where Jacqueline and Betsy sat, watching as a slightly younger man drew Jacqueline to dance once the musician picked up a tune again.

"Why did you come back?" she asked Godfrey.

"Some say he never left," Gunter said. "I've got a theory he was here a year before I heard from him, and that was only 'cause I ran into him on the street. Otherwise we still might not be talking."

"I didn't do a lot of talking then," Godfrey said.

"Godfrey isolated himself," Gunter explained. "It was here or the school. Didn't want to be found so he didn't even give this place a sign. Just wanted a quiet spot for himself and the few people he tolerated. Course, I don't know about quiet," he chuckled, "and over time people found it, little by little."

"Like Jacqueline," said Godfrey.

"Just walked right in one day after five years," Gunter said. "Godfrey dropped his glass. Wouldn't even look at her, and they were practically the only ones in the bar."

"How did she find it?" asked Emile.

"Said she was just passing by. But I think a little birdie told her," Gunter said to Betsy as Betsy joined their group.

Emile glanced over her shoulder at Jacqueline; her head was buried in the chest of the man she danced with.

"She needed friends after that monster," Betsy said.

"He was barely ever there! She had a private cottage in town and a whole ocean to herself."

"And the knowledge of what she'd gotten herself into to sit with. Men like that don't love," Betsy said. "From the moment they married, her husband cheated on her, and when she became too difficult about it he divorced her and threw her out with nothing," she explained. "Humiliated her, sent her back to her parents – they were furious. *He* kept his reputation. She had nowhere else to go."

"I gave her the job," Godfrey defended.

"Teaching *Sensuality.* And then didn't talk to her for years," Betsy said as Gunter laughed and shook his head.

"But things are fine now, aren't they?" said Emile, beholding a lively Jacqueline now sitting beside the musician and laughing. She had never seen signs of a fracture between her and Godfrey's friendship.

"Eventually they reconciled," said Gunter. "It was all many years ago."

"For a long time I vowed I would never be a Fool again like I was for her. But slowly I realized that that was exactly the way to live. I owe Jacqueline much. She was my greatest teacher," Godfrey said with surprising sobriety. "Now I would love to dredge up more old memories, but I must not be a bad host," he slid off his stool and went to join Jacqueline and the musician at their table in the corner.

Gunter sighed. "If you ask me, she wasn't worth all the heartache. You're a real gem," he turned to Betsy. "It's not your fault he's such an idiot."

"You mean a 'Fool'," she replied. Gunter gave a short laugh.

"There's still a chance," he nudged.

"Oh please, catch up. All our chances are long behind us. I don't think I'll be around here for long, anyway."

Gunter gave her a sympathetic look.

"Don't believe the myth, Emile," Betsy turned to her. "For those who spend their entire lives on the playground the rest of us are just supporting characters in their stories. We're two dimensional stereotypes at best."

She took her glass and walked back into the crowd to join Jacqueline, who sat on Godfrey's left while the musician sat on his right. Gunter followed, and Emile, left alone, went last.

"I thought you left!" she cried to the musician.

"I changed my mind," he hiccuped before a number of empty glasses .

"Ha!" Godfrey barked. "I caught this bastard sneaking out at the last second. You think you could leave without a night of revelry with your older brother?" Godfrey threw his arm around the lanky man.

"Your *brother*!?" Emile balked.

"Yes, Adrian is my brother, and it's nice to see him for the first time in five years!"

"I see not much has changed in that time," Adrian looked around the bar.

"*Au contraire*, it hasn't been the same since you left. You can't have *half* of the Clown and the Bard," said Godfrey.

"This is your bar as well?" Emile asked Adrian.

"Indeed I'm the other owner."

"I was the clown and Adrian was the bard," Godfrey smiled. "Adrian used to draw in the crowds in those early days. Unfortunately the town didn't have enough of a drinking problem so I had to take the teaching job at Lom with him."

"*You* taught at Lom?" Emile couldn't believe it.

"Many years ago," said Adrian, flushing somewhat.

"How the students missed you!" Godfrey howled. "There hasn't been a music class since."

"Why did you leave?" asked Emile.

"I came into odds with the new headmaster's principles. Eventually he replaced all the classes with ones from his own curriculum, including mine."

"Don't be so sensitive. I kept music around until the end. As I've always said, I aim to teach kids what they *really* need to know," Godfrey said with force.

"Apparently they don't need to know math," Adrian muttered. "That was the first to go when he became headmaster. He replaced his math class with Foolishness," said Adrian.

"If you can manipulate people well enough they'll do the math *for* you. One of the many things I learned on my travels," Godfrey stated stubbornly. "Everything you learn here I learned too late myself and I paid dearly for it," he said to Emile.

Adrian and Jacqueline shared exasperated looks.

"Why is it so ludicrous? The whole curse of life is that by the time we become wise we've already made our mistakes! Is it such nonsense to try and escape that? No, take it from me, it's best to let the world beat you down as young as you can."

"If only they'd heard that when they hired you," said Adrian flatly.

"I'm a Fool, not an idiot," Godfrey said.

"Really, it was foolish of *me* to be surprised that they were blinded by charisma over years of experience," said Adrian.

"Oh nonsense. You were always the ladies' man. Adrian could have had any girl he wanted, and for some reason he ended up alone, just like his brother."

Adrian shot Jacqueline a half-glance above Godfrey's awareness.

"You could always hire another musician," said Adrian coolly, changing the subject.

"These have no patience for it," Godfrey waved at the students filling his bar. "Except Emile. She's like you, I knew it the moment she walked in. In fact I have no idea how she got here."

"I followed someone," blurted Emile. "I followed a little girl when I got lost one night and she led me here. All those letters I wrote were for her."

"Did you find her again?" Godfrey asked.

"I don't look for her anymore," said Emile. "I think maybe I imagined her."

"Well, regardless of how you got here, you're here now, and if there's one thing I've learned it's to enjoy the moment while it's here," Godfrey said. He took off his jester's hat and rammed it onto Adrian's head.

"Have you ever washed that thing?" Adrian asked with disgust as the hat flattened his curls.

"I don't want to get rid of its essence," Godfrey brushed off as he jumped off his stool and grandly held out his hand to Jacqueline to join him on the floor.

"One last one for me, and make it slow," he directed Adrian to play.

Annoyed, Adrian struck up a slow, pulling ballad.

Emile watched the pair dance, their heads bent in toward each other and their arms around each other. Their eyes were half closed; the rest of the world had been muted.

"Do you think they'll get together now?" Emile asked Gunter, who was leaning against the table watching them.

"We used to place bets. We stopped about ten years ago."

"I don't understand.... What's stopping them?" Emile was unable to fathom it. Happiness stood right next to them, yet they did not take it.

"Themselves," he said. "Perhaps something was lost in the beginning. Perhaps it's better it doesn't happen. Jacqueline's done a number on that family."

"I'm sure she didn't mean to."

"No one ever means to. That didn't stop their father from

detesting her. She was a rich girl, after all, could have anyone she wanted. Why did she want Godfrey? And Godfrey's much older now. He sees things differently."

"How so?"

"That stupid hat he always wears? It was his father's. His only relic of him. He used to be an actor. Favored Godfrey over Adrian, poor kid," Gunter looked at Adrian, who sat playing with his eyes closed. "'Course, in the end Adrian ended up more like him anyway. At least Godfrey could hold something down for more than a year..."

As he trailed off with his memories Emile looked around for Dorian, waiting for him to come by and grab her onto the dance floor again. She glimpsed him colluding out of the way with Lillian, his hand resting on the wall above her shoulder while she leaned her back against the wall, meeting his steady look with a hard gaze of her own. Emile's stomach dropped at the sight of their faces so close together.

The music had stopped and the bar reverted to its usual noisy babble. A very drunk Godfrey stumbled over and fell onto the table.

"I'll tell you a secret, Emile. There's only one person in this town who truly doesn't belong, and that's Adrian. You, you're a mutt. At first I was going to send you to him. How differently things would've turned out for you! But I saw something in you," he scrutinized her face as if trying to see it again.

"What?" she asked.

"I don't remember, I was drunk! Honestly, it might've been a trick of the beer," his smiled, showing all his yellow teeth before collapsing onto the table.

Emile looked around the bar at the same scene she had walked into many months ago. Godfrey snored, occasionally jerking up and swaying on his seat, on the verge of passing out again; his hat had fallen onto the floor and lay there neglected. Betsy and Gunter chatted surreptitiously in a corner, shaking their heads. Lillian and Jesa scampered past her, muttering, "We'll get so many points in Lying and Manipulation!" with excitement, while Dorian had stepped to the side and leaned against the bar for a momentary break. He surveyed the crowd like he owned it, looking both weary and self-satisfied. His face appeared far older than when they had first entered Lom.

On her way out the door Emile passed Jacqueline and Adrian sitting close together in a dark corner, leg to leg, talking in low voices. Adrian directed more focus onto her than he had onto everyone in the school and the bar combined. Jacqueline glanced up at her as she passed while

Adrian, though decently sober, paid her no notice. Jacqueline's eyes fell behind Emile onto Godfrey, passed out early in the night and snoring on a table, and her lips fell, too. Gaunt stood by the doorway in silence, meeting Emile's eyes and saying nothing.

By the morning her bags were packed. She stepped outside the gate. The castle walls were strangely quiet, their usual buzzing whispers gone; the cracks, the windows, the turns around corners that had for months misguided her no longer contained the elusive magic that had made them dance with untraceable motion. The ghost of the potentially existing world they'd maneuvered through had fled, leaving the town just another town.

Emile breathed in the late summer air whose scent called her onward, passing by morning faces going on with life as best as they could. She walked down to the Clown and the Bard early that afternoon; still, above the old door the lantern was unlit.

There sat Godfrey with his back bent over, sipping a beer to stave off his hangover, the yellow cap faithfully on the counter like a dog. Beside him sat Gaunt and Jacqueline, the latter drinking a coffee from a little teacup, still wearing her faded black corset and looking unfocused into the scrubbed counter as if lost in thought and somewhat tired.

She nodded somberly at something said by a younger, pugnacious looking woman bouncing a baby boy behind the counter next to Brody.

"... Maybe in another five years. He's probably somewhere in Romania by now," Godfrey replied.

Jacqueline sympathetically patted his back.

Godfrey shrugged. "Might leave myself in a few years to do the same. Pass on the bar to you," he nodded to Brody, who only replied with, "In a few years you won't want to do anything but sit," as if he'd heard the promise of an aging man too often.

"Basko will be only too thrilled. If you leave his bar will get all your business," Brody's wife tossed her head toward a nearby bar further down the street. "Hold him a minute, he drooled all over me," she handed her son to Jacqueline, who took the baby awkwardly.

"It's just not as fun as it used to be," Jacqueline sighed as she bounced the boy on her lap to keep him from crying. "Everyone's on their way out. Soon Betsy, too."

"Since when?" Godfrey turned to her in surprise.

"It's been in the cards a while. Her mother's not well and once, you know, she's always talked about moving to Prague with some boyfriend," said Jacqueline.

"She'll never do it," said Godfrey.

"Betsy?" Jacqueline countered.

"You might have to do some hiring soon,"added Brody.

"No one can replace Betsy. I'll just take the class off," Godfrey sighed.

"Oh – hush! Sh sh!" Jacqueline bounced the crying child harder, to no effect, and passed him off to Brody.

"Well, I'd better get a move on," said Godfrey, putting his jester's hat on. "*Foolishness* starts in a half hour."

"Want another before you go?" Brody offered.

"Give me another," Godfrey decided and Brody obliged with a fresh beer in one hand and a baby in the other. He glanced over the headmaster at Emile, standing quietly to the side with her bags, and smiled through his beard.

"Are you leaving us?" he asked.

Emile nodded.

"Going back to Locronan?"

"Not just yet," she said.

"Visit anytime," said Godfrey wearily, turning around in his stool. "You're always welcome."

Jacqueline nodded with tired eyes and Gaunt flashed the tiniest lift of his lips. Emile thought of Lillian and Dorian, still

210

asleep in the castle.

"How would I find you again?" she asked.

"On a map," Godfrey snorted at the absurdity of the question. "We're at 24 Brenska Street in Mikulov. Half a day by train from Prague."

The Light to the Light

The story I wanted to write began with the image of a little explorer holding an ancient lantern that creaked as it swung in her hand. She ran through the streets of a beautiful but vague ancient town. The more I chased her, the more intricate the story around her became. People's faces, identities, and stories sprung up like flowers around her feet. Beautiful, intricate stories, succulent dramas that created history. I saw their faces clearly, knew their problems and weaknesses intimately... but I could never pinpoint *her,* the one who drove the story. I only saw her back as I chased her through the winding streets of this imaginary town that had not existed before her.

Out of nothing a world was created. Hundreds of faces and personalities, each particular, filled it. The buildings, bred of imagination, came forth out of stone. The maps and streets, the streetlights and places of worship, cemented into reality. The birth of this town was like a child learning to speak: little by little words accumulated, the language developed, and civilization matured.

All the while I chased the girl with the light to find her role in the story. Her sole existence was the reason for this now rich and vibrant setting. She had led me to an invisible place that lay in the black void of possibility, that infinite pool more terrifying than an ocean, waiting to emerge in its earthly shapes and colors.

Still I kept running, to the farthest edges, and when I reached the end I lost her. She whipped around a corner and I followed her into an empty street. She was nowhere. I searched and searched the now fully animated town, walked every street, peered into every door – but nobody knew her. No one had heard of the source of their own existence. She was a ghost. Just when the town had reached its peak, the possibly existing being with no name or face or identity who began the story disappeared from it altogether, leaving no trace of herself but in her wake a complete world.